Finding
Abigail

CARRIE ANN RYAN

DEDICATION

To my Street Pack who wanted Abby's story
before I knew I wanted it even more.

ACKNOWLEDGMENTS

This was one of my favorite books to write because the people around me wanted it as much as I did. Thank you Lia Davis for helping me and being my right hand.

This book wouldn't have been written without the help and support of my Pack, Tamara, Karen, Jo, Kelly, Fatin, and Lia included. Thank you!

Scott, your covers are amazing. You spent way too much time on this one since I didn't know what I wanted, but thank you so much for finding the model, George. He's my perfect Tyler.

And thank you to my readers. I hope you guys get to enjoy a special Valentine's Day treat and get to love the Coopers as much as you do the Redwood Pack.

Chapter 1

"Valentine's Day is just around the corner. Have you found your love yet?"

Tyler Cooper turned off the radio and cursed. No, of course he hadn't found his love yet. He didn't want to. Who in their right mind would want to be with someone on Valentine's Day? All that love, warmth, and togetherness crap was nauseating. Plus, as soon as someone had a date for Valentine's Day, suddenly warm and fuzzy images entered their minds and visions of wedding bells and engagement rings filled their dreams. It turned into crack for the lovebirds.

It was enough to make a grown man want to lock himself away in his apartment for the entire month of February. Though with the way the Coopers were falling around him, he had to be careful. Matt and Justin were already down for the count with their women; he didn't want to be next. No women for him on that *special* day. No, he'd be in hiding—no, staying in because Coopers didn't hide. Yeah, that sounded like a plan.

Yes, because rationalizing it like that made it *so* much better.

The sun beat down on Tyler's face as he got out of his SUV, and he stopped for a minute to let it warm him. Though the coldness of a Montana winter could seem as bitter as any tundra, the ice seemed to melt away with each passing hour. Ugh, even the weather tried to warm up at the thought of Valentine's Day, didn't it? God, he hated this holiday. Too much pink, too many flowers, too much candy, and too many doe-eyed women who thought they'd 'find the one'. Well, it wasn't going to be him.

A chilled breeze slid past him, seeping into his bones. Though he'd lived in Holiday his entire life, sometimes he wished he lived in a place with a warmer climate; one where his balls didn't feel as though they were icing over every time he had to go outside.

He took a steadying breath, then strolled to the car in front of his SUV. Yeah, never a dull moment in his Montana town. No, Mrs. Ellis, the eighty-eight-year-old busybody had been caught going sixty in a thirty-five. In some states, the woman would already be in jail for that kind of reckless driving. Or at least she should be. Why was it that, in his town, the elderly seemed to be the ones who had lead feet, while everywhere else the geriatric set would drive at a snail's pace, just as they did with their walkers?

Oh, woe was he.

And now he sounded like a damn pansy.

He tapped his notebook on her driver's side window and made a motion with his hand so she'd lower it. She should have known the drill by now. After all, this was the third offense in as many months. Now that the old mayor was out and his new sister-in-law had settled into the role, traffic violations could actually be dealt with and not thrown under the rug with the enticement of money. This meant that Mrs. Ellis would be losing her license this time. It was about damn time. Not only was the paperwork a bitch, but the old lady could have killed someone. He shuddered to think what could have happened if he hadn't caught her.

Again.

"Oh, Sheriff Cooper? What brings you out in this frigid day?" She had the audacity to bat her eyelashes at him underneath her blond, curly-haired wig.

Yeah, like she was fooling anyone about her age with that.

Tyler took a deep breath and lowered his sunglasses. "License and registration, ma'am."

"Oh, dear boy, you don't need those. Why, I helped powder your bottom when you were a baby."

She had done no such thing. She had been too busy sucking up to the old money in town and didn't want to bother with the hard-working Coopers. No matter that the Coopers had more money than most, but that was neither here nor there.

Tyler closed his eyes and prayed for patience. He really needed to stop worrying about what people thought of him and his family. In fact, he didn't really care; he just didn't like liars.

Mrs. Ellis was one of the worst; the ugliest gossip in town, at least on the inside. She'd take the minimal amount of information she could get her little wrinkled hands on and blow it out of proportion so she'd be the center of attention.

God, he hated small towns sometimes.

"Ma'am, I need your license and registration," he said, this time in a firmer tone that didn't quite hide his impatience. If he wanted, he could have her arrested if she continued to refuse, but that was the last thing he needed.

God forbid he had to deal with the glares and upturned noses of the other busybodies if he put their leader behind bars. Though the picture of Mrs. Ellis behind bars in an orange jumpsuit did put a smile on his face. He quickly frowned, so she wouldn't guess what he had been thinking about.

Mrs. Ellis huffed and rolled her eyes. Yes, that was a perfect example of maturity. Or not. She handed him her paperwork then drummed her fingers on her steering wheel. With each staccato beat, his tension increased and his shoulder blades itched. He had no idea why the latter was happening, but it must have something to do with the crazy woman in front of him.

"So, Tyler, dear, are you sure you need to write me a ticket? I wasn't going that fast, was I?" She fluttered her eyelashes again, and Tyler, again, resisted the urge to roll his eyes. He had to remain the adult in this situation.

"Mrs. Ellis, you were going sixty in a thirty-five. You could have killed someone. School's about to let out. How would you have felt if you'd have hit one of those kids because you were going too fast?"

The color drained from her face before she waved her hands. "Oh, I would have stopped for them."

Tyler shook his head and wrote her a ticket. "You don't know that. The laws are in place for a reason. Use them."

Mrs. Ellis turned up the radio and shook her head, clearly wanting to avoid the situation. "Can you believe this? Only two weeks until Valentine's Day, and they're just now working up the dance invitations. In my day we had the whole dance set up after Christmas, and the dates worked out accordingly. There were no stags or lonely ladies home at night, no sir. Now look at it. It's as if people don't care about the holiday at all."

Tyler signed the ticket and handed it to her while trying to tune out her droning voice. He hated this holiday more than most, but really, he had good reasons. He was connected to it more than anyone he knew, and he didn't want to find love. He didn't need it, nor did he want to hear about it.

"So, dear, do you have a date for the dance? Such a young, virile man like you probably has no trouble getting a date." She fluttered her eyelashes again, and Tyler held back the urge to roll his eyes, *again*.

"No, ma'am. I'll probably be working." He handed her the ticket, and she curled a lip in disgust. Not his problem anymore.

"Oh, dear, that just won't do. What would your mother say about you shirking your responsibilities as a handsome man on a night as important as Valentine's Day?"

The sharp, familiar pang at the thought of his mother echoed through him, and he fisted his hands.

"Take care of that ticket, ma'am," he bit out, then turned on his heel and walked backed to his SUV.

That woman had no right bringing up his mother, had no right barging into his life...had no right to anything having to do with him. He watched as she drove off—a little too quickly for his tastes—then closed his eyes.

Thank God that was his last stop. As of five minutes ago, he was officially on a two-week vacation. Yeah, he'd lied that he'd have to work at the dance, but he didn't really care.

A sharp itchiness attacked each of his shoulder blades, and he rubbed his back against his seat like a bear in the forest. Holy fuck it hurt. It had been happening off and on for the past year, and he knew what it was about.

That didn't mean he wanted to think about it. Fuck, everything was catching up with him, and he wasn't ready. He'd had his whole life to be ready, yet everything was coming too fast.

He started his SUV and drove home, scratching his back against the seat as he did so. He was damn lucky he didn't get in an accident. Yeah, that's all he needed, the sheriff getting involved in a collision because he'd been too busy trying to scratch an itch on his back.

Classy.

He pulled up to his apartment complex and turned off the motor, letting his head calm. He ran a hand through his dark, closely shorn hair and sighed.

It wasn't supposed to be like this.

He'd thought he'd have more time before it all caught up with him. But, no, he was a thirty-two-year-old man who had a path to follow that he hadn't wanted.

Fuck. He banged his hand against the steering wheel and shook his head. He sounded like a petulant teenager. He got out of the SUV, slammed the door, and stalked up to his apartment. He nodded at his neighbor as she watered the potted plant the landlord let her keep out.

It wasn't a rundown place by any means, but it wasn't really home. It was more of a waiting place, a purgatory, before he moved on. Yet, he had no idea what he wanted to move on to. He closed the door behind him and set his keys on the table by the door.

He undid his tie and set his hat next to his keys while he looked around the place. He'd painted the walls a cream color, bland and boring, and had kept his college furniture so it looked like the bachelor pad of a man who needed to grow up.

Oh, that was just great. Now he was disparaging his own home. Shit. He stalked toward his fridge, took out a beer, and had swallowed half of it before his headache started to recede. The itch and burn increased on his shoulder blades, and he cursed. He took another drink of his beer then set it down, the pain in his shoulders intensifying.

His body shook, and a cold sweat trailed down his spine as he took wobbly steps toward his living room. He gripped the edge of his couch, his fists bunching the fabric, tearing it at the seams. He felt the veins on his temples bulge, pulse.

Shit, what the hell?

He hadn't though it would hurt this much.

He let go of the couch, his body overheated, needing release. Tyler stripped off his shirt, buttons hitting the ground at his reckless strength. He felt the skin on his back tear and stretch, and something foreign unfurled off his shoulder blades. A slight pain shot through him, then a sudden pleasure like the release after cracking his knuckles slid around him. With each tug and slide, he felt like something was suffocating him—his future altering with each change.

Oh, he knew what it was; he just hadn't wanted to think about it.

He shook, the pain white-hot and blinding, as the wings he'd ignored for so long, hoping they'd never appear, slid out of his back and filled the room.

Finally, oh, God, finally, he calmed, his wings in place, his destiny sealed. Taking a deep breath, Tyler opened his eyes, not ready to look behind him. But, he wasn't a coward; no, he was a Cooper. He risked a glance and cursed.

White wings sprouted out of his back.

He moved them slightly so he could get a better look and cursed again. Yeah, still a bit tender, but wings tearing their way out of a back would do that to a guy.

He looked closer and saw they weren't fully white. No, they had light pink colorization on the edges of each feather and the surface held an even lighter dusting of pink.

Oh, fucking hell. Yeah, that's manly.

Not only did he have wings, they were fucking pink.

"Holy shit, Tyler. What the fuck?" Brayden, his brother, asked as he came into the living room.

Damn it. Why hadn't he locked the door behind him? Served him right for growing up in a family that felt comfortable enough to walk into each other's homes unannounced. He'd never do it at his older brother Jackson's again. Well, maybe. Fuck.

"Tyler? You have fucking wings. Pink-as-fuck wings."

"Why is it people think you're the nice one, Bray?" Tyler asked as he turned toward his brother. His wings knocked a lamp off his side table, and he winced. "Fuck, I'm not used to these things yet."

"People think I'm the nice once because I *am* nice. Just not to you freaks. But, what the hell, Ty?"

"I have issues."

"No shit, but really, what the fuck? They're pink."

Tyler could feel the heat in his cheeks and knew he was blushing. Damn, that's all he needed—his face to match his wings.

"Yeah, well, it comes with the job. And why the hell aren't you freaking out more?" Tyler stood as still as he could and tried to will his wings to go away so he could sit down. No such luck.

Bray shook his head then got a beer out of the fridge. Ah, it was so nice that his brothers felt it was okay to take his shit. Yeah, not so much.

"You ask this after Matt turns into a ghost for eleven years, Jordan is a witch, Justin is one of Santa's friends, and his fiancée is an elf? You being, well, whatever the hell you are, doesn't faze me. It's just one more thing tossed onto the Coopers. We'll deal."

There did seem to be a lightning rod of holiday and other weird crap in the center of their family, though Rina, the elf, said it was the town, not the Coopers, that was the center. Well, that didn't seem entirely accurate if he analyzed what had happened in the past few months.

"What fiancée?" Tyler moved quickly toward Bray and knocked over a picture frame. The glass hit the floor with a crash. "Fuck."

"Smooth, twinkle toes," Bray said as he took the spot on the couch Tyler wanted. Fucker. "That's why I'm here. Justin popped the question, and Rina was doe-eyed enough to say yes."

"Well, hell. We're falling like flies." First Matt had married his high-school sweetheart, Jordan, after she'd come back to Holiday. Now, Justin had his Rina, though he'd already known about Matt, so it shouldn't have been too surprising. At least there were three more Coopers to hold the fort of singlehood.

"Well, with those wings, I'm sure you can stay in the air a bit longer," Bray drawled as he took a swig of his beer. "Now, you gonna tell me what the hell you are?"

"I thought Jordan said it was rude to ask that," Tyler said, delaying the inevitable.

Bray raised a brow. "Jordan isn't here, and you're my brother. What's with the wings?"

"I'm a cupid."

Bray nodded. "I figured since it's February, you have pink wings, and. well, this is *Holiday*, it had something to do with that. Wanna tell me exactly what that means, and why you don't seem surprised by it?"

Tyler shrugged, knocking over a pillow with his wings.

"They're not that pink. And I've known all my life."

"They're pink; don't lie. What the hell, Ty? I thought you got on Matt for lying about being a ghost. Now look at you."

"What happened to Matt was *done* to him. I was born this way."

"So, it's hereditary. Guess that means Jackson and I should be scared."

"No, shit. I don't know." Tyler looked

into his brother's eyes and didn't see surprise at the whole hereditary thing. "Is there something you want to tell me about a holiday you're connected to? Am I missing something?"

"We're talking about you right now," Brayden evaded.

"You're hiding something."

"I'm not in the mood to talk about what is or could be happening. How did you know you were a cupid?" Brayden said as he raised a brow, daring Tyler to continue on the subject that seemed a bit touchy.

"Fine, we'll drop it for now. As for my being a cupid? I just remember hitting puberty and another cupid coming to the house and explaining my job."

"Another cupid? There are more of you?"

"Apparently, it's a business like Justin being Santa's executive. I don't know. I haven't done anything with it and haven't had the wings or anything until now. This is my first year, and I don't know what the fuck I'm doing. They're supposed to send me a packet or some shit explaining where my zone is."

"So, you're supposed to spread...love?"

Tyler sighed and winced as his wings went back to being hidden, sliding back into his skin, folding with a slight creak in his bones. It felt as though someone was bending his arm at an odd angle, not hurting, but not feeling like he wanted to do it every day either. Apparently, all he had to do was relax while thinking about making his wings disappear. Nice, he'd have to remember how he did that for the next time.

"I suppose it's my job to help people find their true love."

"You? Mr. I-don't-make-commitments-past-breakfast?"

"Yep. Pretty much. Now, if you'll excuse me, I need a nap before I deal with the fact that I'm a fucking cupid, and don't know what the hell I'm doing."

"A nap? Really? That's all you have to say? Damn, Tyler. You don't even want to think about getting married. How are you supposed to help others?"

"I don't fucking know. It's my job, my...destiny. We'll see what happens when the packet comes and I figure out what to do, but I don't know."

"So, you can tell when people are supposed to be together?" Bray asked, nervousness in his tone.

Oh, he knew his brother had a right to be nervous, but it didn't take him being a cupid to know who Bray should be with considering his brother never had eyes for anyone other than Allison. But that was another story.

"Those powers will come now that I've reached cupid-maturity, or whatever they called it."

Bray let out a breath then got up to leave. "Are you going to tell the others?"

"I don't have a choice, do I? I mean, you know."

"I can keep a secret if you need me to, but I think the others should know."

Ty let out a breath and finally sat on the couch. "Yeah, I'll tell them. As soon as I know what the hell I'm doing."

Bray let out a dry laugh. "You might want to tell them before that. Since if you wait that long, we'll all be dead."

"Ass."

"You want me to just let them know?"

Relief filled him. "Sure, that way I can just deal with the questions later. Because you know there'll be tons."

Bray smiled, and Tyler shook his head. "Does this mean you can find your own true love?"

An odd hollowness spread through Tyler at the thought. "I don't know."

Bray nodded, his eyes a little too knowing. "Okay then, twinkle-toes. Keep the wings hidden, and I'm here if you need me." His brother let himself out, and Tyler laid down on the couch.

Well, hell. Now his brothers would know and, in turn, the women and their group of friends. Secrets didn't go over well in the Cooper family, even though they all had them. He'd known since he was a kid what he'd have to become, that he'd finally arrive at that special age to be the cupid of Holiday and wherever the hell else they sent him. That he'd have to be the man, cupid, whatever, to expose love in people's hearts.

What if he didn't want to? After all, he didn't believe in love. It wasn't for him, and there damn sure wasn't a woman for him. Not in Holiday, not anywhere.

Chapter 2

How many skeins of yarn does a person need to collect before it became hoarding and not just there for a rainy day?

Abigail Clarke shook her head at her own question and started to throw various colors and textures of yarn into a canvas bag. Instead of trekking to her new place with them in tow, she'd just donate them to the Holiday Women's Society since they knitted more than she did anyway. Dear Lord, she was twenty-two and a closet knitter. Even though she'd been living like an adult since she was fourteen, she was still a baby compared to most of her friends.

And, she was still a closet knitter.

Okay, not so much in the closet since the whole town thought she *only* knitted, baked, and cleaned her little house. God forbid they imagine her with a life of her own where she got to at least have some semblance of fun.

So, what if they were partially correct?

Abby stuffed the last skein in the back and curled her lip. Partially? More like fully these days. This was supposed to be the time of her life, right? Then why did she have so much freaking yarn? Oh, yeah, because at the tender age of twenty-two, she was turning into a recluse. A leper. A freaking one woman pity-party of fun. Yay, freaking, yay, for her.

Thank God she was moving. She needed to put this town and their attitudes in the past. Yes, she was only twenty-two, but she'd been lucky in her schooling and had graduated early while taking college courses at the same time. She'd done it all too quickly so she could get on with her life, always feeling like she was older than her years.

By the time she was eighteen, she'd already finished most of her college courses and was ready to start working alongside other teachers so she could get her teaching certificate. So, by the time she reached twenty, she was ready to be a full time teacher.

She knew it was stupid to leave after only two years of teaching to move, but if she didn't do it now, she might not ever do it...

She needed a new life, one where people didn't see her and automatically think "virgin school-teacher" or "brainiac."

So what if they were right? That didn't mean it was okay to put her in that little box and never let her out. How was she supposed to grow and find her own way if everyone knew *everything* about her and her history? Like how she'd never had a boyfriend. Okay, let's be serious... she'd never even had a date.

Yep, Abby was epidemically dateless.

Why was she perpetuating the stereotype? A schoolteacher, a virgin, a closet-knitter... Oh, and she couldn't forget the curves and her sweet tooth. She grinned as she popped a candy heart in her mouth. Its chalkiness melted on her tongue, and she smiled. At least Valentine's Day gave her candy, even if she couldn't get a date and bought it herself.

The town thought she was the cat-lady without the cats.

Well, screw them.

They didn't know she danced like a wanton when she wanted to or that she had every type of clit-stimulator known to man that didn't penetrate because, for some reason, she wanted to keep her actual virginity intact.

No, they didn't know that.

A blush spread over her, and she laughed. Yeah, she didn't necessarily want them to know that last part, but it would at least be nice if they thought she *could* own those things. But, no, she was sure if the town ever found out, they'd have a collective heart attack. All of them. Just a mass collapse of the townsfolk as they learned little Abby liked it rough—or at least *wanted* it rough.

Abby smiled at that thought.

Okay, not the whole death thing, but all of them collectively passing out would be amusing. Maybe she should strut down Main Street in her dancing clothes...the jeans that hugged her rounded curves and the shirt that covered her stomach, but made her boobs look like a place to shelve things.

Yeah, that would scare the crap out of the town.

And, she'd still end up going home alone because there wasn't anyone here for her. No one gave her another look past seeing her as a schoolteacher. Other than the Cooper brothers, no one *knew* her. And the Coopers thought of her like a sister.

Abby let out a sigh then ate another candy while she packed up another stack of romance novels to take with her.

She liked being their "sister." The Coopers were better than any big brothers she could have had. They were nice, sexy, and took care of each other. They didn't even pick on her like a real brother would, at least not beyond the normal teasing.

Well, at least Matt, Justin, Brayden, and Jackson did anyway.

Tyler, on the other hand...

Tears prickled her eyes, and she blinked them away, pissed off at herself beyond belief. Why the heck was she crying? Just because she'd loved the man since she was six, she didn't have to fall into a weeping puddle at the thought of him.

God, how pathetic could she get? She loved—no, not somewhat liked or crushed on— a man who didn't *see* her. He didn't really ever acknowledge her existence. She was just...there. A fixture in his day-to-day life that she was sure didn't mean anything.

And, she freaking loved him.

She wasn't one of those teenagers who pined over their unrequited loves. No, she'd grown past that once she hit her twenties.

Yes, the irony of the short time frame in which she hadn't acted like a doe-eyed Twi- hard for the sheriff of Holiday didn't escape her. She didn't think of him as a god or perfect.

She snorted.

No, there was no *way* the man could be classified as perfect.

But she'd always had some form of hope that he'd *see* her. That he'd finally realize the woman he could spend the rest of his life with was standing right next him, immersed in his family, not because she stalked him, but because they loved her like she loved them. He'd realize the woman who could help him find his happiness was just one dance away.

But that never happened.

At first, she'd thought it was the ten-year age difference. In reality, that was a problem for most. And, yes, she'd loved him since she was six. It had started as a crush of a six-year-old girl who'd fallen off her bike. Instead of going to her parents, who'd have just ignored her and kept fighting, she'd stayed on the curb, waiting for the pain to go away.

Then a dreamboat by the name of Tyler Cooper had sat down next to her without saying anything. He'd been sixteen and an older man in her little eyes. He'd cleaned out her wound and put a Band-Aid on it. He'd, apparently, witnessed her fall from grace and had run home to get what he might need to help her. He'd kissed her knee and told her she was brave.

That had been the last time he'd noticed

her beyond the casual hello or help with work.

The last time she'd felt his lips anywhere near her.

No, Mr. One-Night-is-Enough kept finding women from out of town to....well, yeah. Abby didn't even rate a placement on his long line of potential...dates. Nope, she was just Abby.

Nothing to him.

Well, dammit, that didn't mean she was *nothing* to herself.

She laughed because the double negatives hurt her head. No, she was smarter than the girls in those movies. She'd long since given up thinking he would drop everything one day and suddenly want her. No, Abby hadn't put all of her hopes in thinking he'd love her.

Abby wasn't moving away from Holiday to run from Tyler Cooper. She was moving because there wasn't anything left for her here. She had her friends and her job. That was it. Unless there was a sudden influx of eligible bachelors, the town had run dry of men who might eventually want her.

And, by run dry, she meant there hadn't been any at all.

It was tough to think like that, even in a town as small as hers, but there wasn't *any* man who might want to marry her. There wasn't even a man who wanted to casually date her. She was tired of living alone—of being alone.

It wasn't as if she hadn't tried. No, she'd finally gotten over her fear of rejection and asked out not one, not two, but five men in town and had been turned down every time. Each one had seemed a little more pitying than the last.

To others, five rejections wouldn't have been that bad, but no one was asking her out either. And yes, she didn't need a man to complete her life, but she didn't want to live in a place where pity was the only thing she received. Even in her friends' eyes, like Jordan Cross, her witchy best friend, pity held a firm grip. Abby knew Jordan tried to hide it, but it was there all the same.

Jeez, she needed to stop feeling sorry for herself. She wasn't running away. Okay, maybe she was, but whatever. She told herself she was moving on and changing her life. There was a difference.

If her house didn't sell, she wasn't moving very far. She'd stupidly bought the thing two years ago when she'd graduated college because the price had been right and she had been ready to start her new life. She'd gotten lucky with scholarships and had saved every penny she had, plus the meager inheritance her grandmother had left her, to put a down payment on her little home with enough land to build on when she married.

Abby shouldn't have thought that far ahead because this was Holiday where the prices were down on homes because no one ever moved in. People didn't want to move to a place in the middle of nowhere where the jobs were set in stone through family and necessity, not development. No one wanted to buy her house because everyone was happy where they were.

The sound of the doorbell startled her out of her misery, and she quickly went to the door, checking herself for crumbs from the cookie she'd eaten earlier in the day. Yeah, that was a great way to stay healthy, in a *not* sort of way.

"I can't believe you're moving," Jordan

said as she walked into the room before Abby even had a chance to welcome her in. "I mean, I just moved back, and we're friends, and you're moving." Jordan stopped and winced. "Well, didn't that just sound selfish and ridiculous? But, seriously, you can't move; Holiday is your home."

Abby smiled at her friend's spirit. There was no holding back for Jordan anymore, not since her friend had finally come to terms with being a witch.

"I need a change, Jor; you know this."

"Can't you just do what you have to here? Why do you have to move to *Denver* of all places?" Jordan spat out the word like the big city wasn't good enough for them. Ironic since Jordan herself had spent the past eleven years or so in New York City of all places. Talk about a life change.

"You know I can't, Jordan."

Jordan rolled her eyes then sat down on the couch among the bags of yarn. Her friend wrapped a string round her finger, her gaze on the motion rather than facing Abby. "Yes, you can. Just because those guys are freaking idiots doesn't mean you can't have what you want."

Abby shook her head and gave a wry smile. "You know that's not true. I need to distance myself from plain-old Abby, and grow up."

"You *are* grown, Abby, dear. You're amazing. I don't know why you don't see that."

"But, that's just it. I *do* see that. I know I'm amazing and that people should get over the past and see that I'm an adult who likes to dance and not just knit. They need to get over the fact that my parents always fought and don't even know who I am anymore. They need to know that I'm not the goody-goody they think I am. But that's not going to happen in a town where everyone knows the exact brand of tampons I use and when I need to buy them."

Jordan curled a lip and shook her head. "That's just sick. You know, that was one part of small-town living I didn't miss."

"Yeah, just wait until they make a connection to when you *stop* buying them. Because believe me, they're watching to see when you and Matt make a mini Cooper." She laughed at her own joke, even as Jordan's eyes widened.

"You're kidding, right? We just got

married."

Abby smiled. "Oh, honey, they even have gossip over whether the baby will be a witch or not. There's a poll over whether you and Matt waited until your vows to start, shall we say, procreating like bunnies. Same with Rina and Justin, and it'll last until they get married. Then the baby monitoring will start all over again for the new couple." She'd heard of the engagement, and though she'd been happy, it still made her ache just that little bit.

Jordan covered her face with her hands. "You're not serious."

"Why do you act surprised? This is nothing new. I love this town sometimes, but not always." Abby put on her serious face and took a deep breath. "I need to move on, Jordan."

Jordan's eyes filled, and she sniffed. "Damn it. I don't want you to go."

Abby cried right along with her. "I don't particularly want to move away from all of you, but there's no room for me to grow here."

"And if you found a man here... would you stay?"

Abby frowned, not liking the reminder that she was leaving for a man, or rather, lack of a man, but that was the point, wasn't it?

"It would have to be more than a man. It would have to be a future. I'm not alive here, Jordan. You, Rina, and the Coopers are what keep me going. Even working at the school is too much sometimes because I know, if I stay here, I'm never going to have a baby of my own. I want a family, a future, just...everything. I don't need a man to complete me. I need a chance. That's the difference."

Jordan sighed and closed her eyes. "I wish I could just magically whip up a man for you, and then you could stay."

Abby laughed, imagining Jordan dressed all in black with a pointy hat, standing over a cauldron, adding a pinch of alphaness, a dash of darkness, a hint of sandalwood and spice.

It didn't escape her notice she was imagining the ingredients that would make up Tyler. She needed help.

Tyler didn't want her, and she'd be okay. She'd move on and find that future and possibility she desperately needed. Darn it, why couldn't the sheriff love her?

Chapter 3

The package didn't seem too dangerous. No, in fact, it looked downright boring. Then why couldn't Tyler open the damn thing? It'd arrived as a special delivery on his doorstep that afternoon like a glaring reminder of his duties.

It'd been three days since his wings had

come in, and all he'd managed to do was learn to keep them in his back so he didn't scare the townsfolk. He could just imagine the looks on people's faces as he strolled down Main Street with wings—*pink fucking wings*.

Though the town was a hub of holiday magical activities and paranormals, not everyone knew to what extent. Sure, they all knew Jordan was a witch. They'd known since she was a child because it was hereditary and her aunt had been one as well, though not to the extent Jordan was. According to Rina, the town had always had magical activities in and around town, but most people had ignored it. This year, everything was coming to light and the townsfolk weren't always forgiving.

The town had gotten its first taste of something *different* and had shunned her, tormented her. The Coopers had stood by Jordan, but that hadn't made a difference, and Jordan had left, heartbroken and just plain broken. When Jordan's aunt had died, Jordan had come back to Holiday and had rekindled her romance with Matt.

Thank God.

Tyler hadn't known how much Matt had needed her in his life until she came back and

Matt had smiled again. In retrospect, his younger brother's sullenness may have had something to do with the fact that Matt had also been a ghost for the previous eleven years.

It had taken several things to break the curse, or whatever it was—Matt fighting for something other than himself and saving Jordan's life.

A secret that big might have been hidden when Matt had been the ghost, but it couldn't be any longer. The rumors had circulated, mere whispers turning into bold questions, and Matt's translucent proclivities had been outed. Yet, the town had just nodded and gone about their business.

Then when Justin and Rina had saved the town from Jack Frost at the children's Christmas play, the town's rumblings had begun again. Only the Coopers and their small group of friends knew that Justin was Santa's executive, the man behind the scenes to help spread holiday cheer and that Rina was one of the elves from the North Pole.

However, the town had made their guesses, and most were spot on. Not that the Coopers would alleviate their curiosity entirely. No, they preferred to keep to themselves.

Tyler wasn't any different. Brayden and, by now, the rest of his family, and most likely their close-knit friends, knew what he was. At least they knew the title, but even he didn't know what his new position meant. The package on the counter in front of him would tell him exactly what it meant to be a cupid.

For instance, would he have to fly around wearing a diaper?

Tyler shuddered at the thought. He hadn't tried flying yet. His back was too tender to even lift his wings fully off the floor for long periods, let alone carry his entire body off the ground. He didn't even want to think about prancing around in a diaper.

And it would be prancing. There was no way he could stroll casually wearing that getup. Jesus, hopefully there wasn't a uniform. Maybe he could just wear jeans and a T-shirt and do what he had to do.

Whatever the hell that was.

He continued to stare at the package and took a deep breath. He could do this. It wasn't as if he could run away. He'd known it was coming, even if he hadn't wanted it. He ripped off the tape and opened the box, his pulse increasing with each movement that brought him one step closer to his destiny.

He took out the card with his name on it and ripped the seal, the scent of vanilla attacking his nose. Great, now he smelled like a fucking cookie. He didn't bother looking at what lay beneath the card; he'd find out soon enough.

Dear Tyler,

Welcome to the art of being a cupid. We know you hadn't wanted this when it was thrust upon you, but we know you will do your job perfectly.

Now, what is your job? Well, that's easy.

You feel that pull in your heart? That tingly sensation when you're around two people who don't realize they're perfect for each other?

Well, that's the beginning of a bond. Not everyone will have it. Not everyone will need you.

But, when you feel that, use your arrow (included) and your bow (also included, isn't it nice how that works?) and strike the one who pulls you more.

You see, the one who pulls at you more needs the bigger push. They're the ones with clouds in their eyes when it comes to finding their one true love.

Yes, you may think it sounds dorky—we know what you're thinking, Tyler, dear—but it's perfect for us.

We cupids come from a long line of love enthusiasts, and we're here to make sure the love in the world is rich and fulfilled. Now, be careful with those arrows.

One prick, and you'll have the overwhelming urge to search for your one true love. You wouldn't want to do that since it could interfere with your job and may scare the person you could fall in love with.

We believe in you.

Love and every ooey-gooey feeling that comes with it,

Frank, head cupid.

"Frank? Who the hell names a cupid Frank?" Tyler read down to the postscript and snorted.

P.S. My parents weren't imaginative with my name. Deal with it. At least I'm not alone. Have fun with those arrows!

Tyler glanced over his shoulder. Okay, this Frank dude was a little creepy. Or maybe Tyler's reaction was normal when it came to the job and all it entailed.

So, his job was to prance around and hit people with arrows? Oh, God, were there tights involved? He peered into the package, but he couldn't see anything else without unwrapping it further.

Please, no tights. Oh, and no diapers.

Tyler took off the last of the brown paper that smelled of vanilla and choked.

Pink. Hot pink. Everywhere.

The arrows were light pink with hearts, all tucked in a hot-pink quiver.

Oh, God. Hell no.

How the hell was he supposed to do this? He was a cupid, sure, but God... pink? Why the hell did it have to be pink?

He took a deep breath and grabbed the quiver. It crinkled under his hand, and he frowned. He took a closer look and laughed.

Plastic wrap. Pink fucking plastic wrap.

He took off a note that he hadn't seen before and smiled.

Sorry, couldn't help myself. It's white, though we're thinking of making a more manly black or slate one. Check back next year.

Okay, so Frank sounded more and more like one of his brothers. Tyler could do this. There didn't seem to be anything else other than the arrows, bow, and quiver in the box. Thank God. But, how the hell was he supposed to go around with it without people noticing?

He looked in the box again and found one last note.

Only you and your beloved can see the bow, arrow, and quiver. That means, even if you don't already know it, the one person, besides you, who can see the evidence of your being a cupid is your one true love. The world won't notice if you're prancing around with it on. You're fine. Good luck, and happy shooting!

Well then.

There would be no prancing.

Tyler took off the wrapping and hooked the strap around his chest. Then he held the bow in his hand and felt warmth spread through him. He blinked as he caught his reflection in the mirror on the wall beside him. Nothing was there. It was as if he wasn't holding the bow and didn't have the quiver on his back.

Dude, this is pretty cool. At least it didn't come with tights.

A sudden tug at his heart startled him. Oh, maybe that was what he was supposed to be feeling. Was he supposed to follow it?

Hell, he really didn't want to do this. Why couldn't he just enjoy his vacation like a normal person? No, he had to be a fucking Cooper and be swallowed whole by the paranormal world.

Okay, he could do this. He *had* to do this.

He left the house and started walking toward the tug, or whatever the hell he was going to call it. He passed by a few people and nodded. They didn't give him any weird looks, so it seemed as though Frank had been right—

they couldn't see the bow, quiver, and arrow. That at least was a good thing. He kept walking until he made his way to his apartment building's gym.

Tony, one of his other neighbors, was frowning at Jessica, the apartment receptionist. His heart tugged harder toward Jessica, and Tyler held back a grin.

Apparently, Jessica was the hard head in this relationship; and people thought men were the hard cases.

He looked around him, and luckily, only one other person was in the room with them so he could maybe hide and hit the two lovebirds with an arrow or whatever he was supposed to do. Unfortunately, the person who stood next to him was Clara, the very married neighbor who kept trying to grab his junk.

He hated that woman.

"Oh, Tyler," Clara purred, "you're here. I can help spot you if you want."

He swallowed the bile that rose in his throat and shook his head. "I saw your husband earlier looking for you," he lied. "I'd go find him if I were you."

She gave him a stormy look and flounced off.

Thank God he'd never slept with her—before or after her marriage. Not that he'd ever sleep with a married woman, but still. He could imagine how clingy she'd be if he had.

Jessica and Tony nodded at him, and he smiled, clearly aware he was still in jeans and looked out of place at the gym. He went to the back and hid behind a pillar.

He rolled his eyes. Yep, this was discreet. Years of training in law enforcement were clearly paying off.

He pulled out an arrow and aimed his bow toward Jessica. Hopefully the arrow wouldn't become visible once it was away from his body. That wouldn't be awkward at all...

Tyler released the arrow, and it flew through the air and hit Jessica's butt—*nice aim*. She jumped, her eyes wide, and Tyler held back a curse. Fuck, that didn't look good.

But, as soon as he was about to turn tail and run, Jessica smiled, and Tony and Tyler froze. He could have sworn he saw a pink ribbon flair from Jessica to Tony's heart. She leaned into Tony, and he traced a finger down her jaw. Tyler couldn't hear what they were saying, but he felt as though he was intruding.

As quietly as he could, he left the building, just as Tony leaned down for a kiss.

The tug on Tyler's heart lessened, and he smiled. Mission accomplished.

He'd just gotten back into his apartment and taken off his quiver when someone knocked on the door.

Who the hell could that be? Hopefully, it wasn't Clara. He shuddered. *Please, don't let it be Clara.*

He opened the door and froze.

Abigail.

"What are you doing here?" he grunted.

"Hello to you too," she said as she made her way into his house without an invitation.

He closed the door and scratched his head. This didn't sound like her at all. In fact, Abigail was usually very timid around him. Not that he really noticed her beyond that.

"What's going on, Abigail?"

"Why do you call me that? Everyone else calls me, Abby." She bit her lip, and his eyes focused on them for a second.

They looked sexy...

He blinked, a gray haze coming over his mind.

Wait. What had he been thinking about?

"Ty? Why do you call be Abigail?"

"It's your name, isn't it?" And he liked the sound of it on his tongue. That gray haze came back, and he rubbed his temples. What the hell?

She shook her head. "Whatever. I'm here to say goodbye actually."

"Goodbye?"

"I'm moving, and I thought I'd say goodbye to all the Coopers." She blinked and looked around as though trying to come up with what to say.

"Moving? Why would you do that?"

"There's nothing for me here."

But, what about...

He closed his eyes as a headache slammed into him.

"What's wrong, Ty?" Abigail walked toward him, and he took a step back. Hurt crossed her face for a moment, her eyes widening as she bit her lip, but then she managed to mask it.

"I'm fine. Just a headache. Uh, I'm sorry to see you go."

Hurt flashed again, and this time, it looked even more painful. Her eyes took on a glassy glaze, almost as if she was about to cry, but she held it back.

"I see." She looked away from his face, and he frowned.

Why was she acting like this?

"What are these?" Abigail asked as she touched his arrows.

Holy shit. How could she see those? Only other cupids and his true love could see them. But, she wasn't his true love; he didn't feel it, even though he felt a little off around her. Was she another cupid?

"What do you see, Abigail?" he asked

carefully.

Her brows rose, and she gave him a "really?" look. "Arrows. That's why I asked you what they were since I didn't think you were a marksman with anything other than the gun that's usually at your hip."

"Here, give me that," he said as he took the quiver full of arrows from her. He reached too fast and swore as one of the arrow tips cut into his hand.

He sucked on his finger, and Tyler almost fell to his knees.

Abigail.

His heart constricted as he saw Abigail for what seemed like the first time.

Luscious curves that were made for his hands called to him. Her breasts were heavy, more than enough for a large handful. Her hips flared out, and he could see himself thrusting in and out of her as he tugged on her hair, keeping her in place.

Long eyelashes framed hazel eyes that looked as if they could see into the very depths of his soul. Shoulder-length brown hair with blunt bangs made her face look innocent, pure.

His.

What the fuck?

How had he not seen her before?

The arrow.

Shit. Abigail was his?

How could he not have known? Something else was at play here, and he didn't know what it was. What he did know was that he suddenly wanted Abigail.

Naked.

Now.

"Why are you looking at me like that?" she asked, her eyes wide. "I'm sorry. I didn't mean to hurt you." She tried to walk around him, but he grabbed her arm, blocking her.

"No, don't go."

"Why? You never wanted me to stay before."

He traced her jaw, and he smiled because her soft, soft skin felt smooth under his finger. "Abigail."

"What's going on? Why are you acting

like this?"

"Go out to dinner with me." *Then stay forever.*

Whoa. Holy shit. Maybe not forever. He didn't do that. He gulped. Did he? *First make her stay for dinner then we can talk about the future.*

What the hell was on that arrow? Some kind of commitment poison?

"What?" she asked, her eyes wide, disbelieving.

"I want you, Abigail."

She pulled back, and confusion and anger warred on her face. "You've got to be kidding me. Now? I'm leaving, Tyler. You've never wanted me before. I'm not a pity date. Fuck you, Tyler Cooper. Just because you didn't want me when I was available doesn't mean others don't either. Don't play games with me."

With one last look, she stormed off and slammed the door behind her.

Holy hell.

Abigail Clarke was the one for him. Why

hadn't he known it before? Something was wrong. Something had held him back. But what? And how the hell was he going to make Abigail stay for him?

He'd just found her, even though she'd been here all this time. He couldn't lose her now, not his Abigail.

Chapter 4

Even after twenty-four hours, Abby was still mad as hell, as well as confused. Also needy and slightly optimistic—which made her even angrier. This couldn't be happening. Tyler Cooper couldn't want her right when she was moving. What kind of cruel joke was he playing?

Her heart ached at the thought.

Why couldn't he have just let her go? He'd already broken her by dismissing her for years, so why add to the misery? She'd gone over there on a whim—a careless one at that. Abby hadn't meant to even go there. She'd just found her car parked in his parking lot as if her body had subconsciously done it.

She'd just wanted to say goodbye. Okay, fine, if she were honest with herself, she'd really wanted him to tell her not to go and say he'd always loved her, but he hadn't—not at first.

Then all of a sudden he'd seemed to want her?

What the hell was that about? It made no sense. She was just Abby. No, not just Abby. She was *Abigail* to him. Still, no matter what he'd said now, she'd always been nothing to him.

Abigail. She liked how it sounded when it rolled off his tongue. Sweet, yet sort of sinful in all the best ways.

She mentally slapped herself. Geez, he didn't really want her. He just wanted to make sure he boinked the only girl in town he hadn't had before she left. Well, that was slightly exaggerating his prowess, but whatever.

Someone slammed a car door, and she blinked. Damn, now she was acting like a freak sitting out in her car talking with herself. Abby got out of the car and made her way into the diner.

She'd promised Allison she'd come in and eat lunch with her and the kids before she left. It had been an entire day since Tyler had made his proclamations—however truthful they were—and he still hadn't contacted her. That just confirmed her fears; he didn't want her.

Whatever. That wasn't new. It was just life.

"Abby! You're here!" Lacy, Allison's youngest, yelled as she ran over to her.

Abby held out her arms and pulled the little girl in tightly. God, she was going to miss this family. She ran hands over six-year-old Lacy's adorable little pigtails and smiled.

"It's good to see you too, pumpkin."

"You're going to eat with us, right? Brayden is already here, so you can eat with all of us." Lacy pulled Abby to where Tyler's brother, Brayden, sat.

Brayden looked like the grungier—in the nicest of ways—version of the Cooper brothers. He was the town mechanic and hopelessly in love with Allison, a widow and mother of three kids, though no one actually thought Brayden knew he was in love. At some point, he'd have to figure it out. Right?

Apparently, the Coopers were a little crazy when it came to feelings and women.

Brayden sat in the booth across from Allison's other two kids, eight-year-old Cameron and twelve year-old Aiden. Both boys looked like their late father, something that haunted Allison, though Abby didn't know why. It was her friend's secret though, and Abby didn't want to pry into it unless invited.

"I see Lacy found you," Allison said with a smile as she carried a tray of waters to another table in the diner. Allison was the head waitress and very good at her job, though the town knew she hated it. But, she'd given up college and any dreams she may have had when she'd married Greg and had Aiden at eighteen.

"Yep, she's determined," Abby said.

Abby laughed and sat down next to the

boys so Lacy could sit next to Brayden. Brayden gave Abby a nod and wrapped his arm around Lacy. Lacy squealed and sank into Brayden's hold. That annoying little maternal clock chimed within Abby, and she held back a sigh. She might have only been in her early twenties, but she was ready for a family. She wasn't like the normal twenty-somethings who wanted to party or find themselves.

She knew what she wanted. She just couldn't get it. Not in Holiday.

God, Brayden looked so good with Lacy in his arms—like a loving father. He said something to the boys, and they laughed and shook their heads. Why couldn't Brayden see he was perfect for this family? Why couldn't Allison and Brayden just tell each other how they felt?

Oh, yeah, like she was one to talk.

She'd had the opportunity the day before, and she'd run from it. But, honestly, it wasn't as if Tyler had been sincere. He probably just wanted a goodbye boink before she left town. Dear Lord, why did she keep calling it boinking? Talk about sounding innocent.

Why did everything have to be so hard? She wasn't an idiot. She knew she wasn't as beautiful as other women out there, but she wasn't ugly by any means. She might be overweight by Hollywood's standard, but she wasn't fat—she *knew* that. Yet why hadn't Tyler shown any interest before she'd told him she'd be unattainable?

Was that the why of it? Maybe he'd offered to take her out to dinner and touched her face in that loving gesture because he knew he couldn't have her. God, what the hell was wrong with her? And what was with those arrows?

They looked like a prop for Cupid. She knew the kids weren't holding a play this semester, even though she wasn't teaching. She'd taken a leave of absence for the semester while she packed and tried to sell her house.

Why on earth would Tyler have arrows with little hearts on them? It wasn't as if he were *the* Cupid...right?

"Everything okay, Abby?" Brayden asked, drawing her out of her thoughts about Tyler yet again.

It was silly, right? Tyler couldn't be

Cupid. Though Justin *was* Santa's helper, and Rina *was* an elf, not to mention Jordan being a witch and Matt being a former ghost.

Maybe it wasn't all that farfetched.

"Abby?"

She shook her head and smiled. "Sorry, I'm spacing."

Brayden frowned. "Because of the move? You don't have to go, Abby. We like you here."

Just not enough. No, that wasn't fair. Her friends were amazing and loved her, but she needed more than that. She *deserved* more than that.

"I need to move, Brayden," she said, choosing to talk about the last part of what he'd said and ignoring the question of what she was thinking about. Brayden didn't need to know her suspicions concerning Tyler, even though it made no sense at all why she'd even think that. It was probably just a prop for some sex game he'd play with his Valentine's date.

Oh, great. That was something she really didn't want to think about.

"Okay, now you look sick, Abby. What's

going on?" Brayden asked.

"Yeah, Abby, what's wrong? Do you want some of my water?" Aiden asked as he leaned closer, concern on his face.

She smiled and ran a hand through his too-long hair that seemed to be in fashion these days. God, she sounded older than twenty-two.

"I'm okay, really. I just have so many things going on in my mind right now, so it's a bit crazy."

"Then don't go," Cameron said as he leaned over Aiden to pat her hand. "Please? We don't want you to leave. It's bad enough you're not at school anymore. Don't leave us."

Tears welled in her eyes, and she brought both boys into a hug. "Oh, guys, you know how much I love you, but I need to go."

"Why?" Lacy said as she leaned into Brayden's hold, tears running down her cheeks.

"Because I need to grow up," Abby said as she fought the battle with her own tears.

She looked up at Brayden, who shook his head. He didn't seem as though he wanted to run away from two crying girls, so a point for him.

"You can grow up right here," Aiden said. "I am."

Abby sniffed and kissed the tops of both boys' heads. "I'm moving, but I'm not leaving your lives forever. I'm still going to visit, and we can talk on the phone and Skype. I promise."

"You promise?" Cameron asked as he fought off tears like a growing boy would.

"I promise, honey."

"It's not the same," Lacy said as she wiped the tears from her face.

"No, it's not, but we're going to make it the best we can."

"How about we get something to eat?" Brayden asked, diffusing some of the tension around the table. He tilted his head toward the diner, and Abby's eyes widened.

Everyone was staring at them, trying to listen to what they were saying. Great, gotta love a small town.

Abby put on her brave face and waved. "We're okay," she lied.

The others didn't look as though they believed her, but most turned back to their meals.

Allison came over, tears in her eyes as well. "Okay, you guys. You're making me weepy, and I need to work." She smiled to take the bite off her words. "I ordered everyone the special—club sandwiches with fries. I hope that's okay."

"Sounds perfect," Brayden said, his eyes on Allison.

How on earth did Allison not know Brayden was in love with her and vice versa? It was so clear in their eyes that Abby was pretty sure even Aiden knew what was going on.

"Thanks, Mom," Aiden said with an odd look on his face, his gaze going between Allison and Brayden.

Abby hugged Aiden harder, and he smiled up at her. Yeah, the kid knew, but he was doing what the rest of the town was doing and letting nature run its course.

Allison blinked at Brayden then smiled at the rest of the table and walked to the back. Abby shook her head. At least she wasn't the only one going through random relationship crap. If she could even call what Tyler had said to her the day before relationship crap.

Probably not since they had no real relationship.

Allison came back with their meals then went back to work. The rest of them ate, talked about Denver, and what Valentines the kids were going to buy to bring to school. Oh, those were the days. A shoebox full of Valentines filled with candy hearts. Why couldn't it be as easy now as it had been back then?

"Abby?" Cameron asked. "Who's your Valentine?"

Abby choked on her sandwich and forced it down with a drink of water. She looked into Brayden's laughing eyes, and she wanted to throw something at that smug face. Not that he looked like a jerk. He just looked like a brother enjoying his sister's discomfort.

"I don't have one, Cam, I'm not really looking," she lied.

Cameron bit on his lip and looked deep in thought. "Well, we'll find you someone. We already picked out Brayden for Momma, so you can't have him, sorry."

This time it was Brayden who choked, and Abby raised a brow. *See? It's not so much fun when it's pointed at you, is it?*

Abby didn't want Bray to feel as though he were drowning for too long, so she saved them both. "Why don't you worry about your own Valentine, Cam, and leave the adults to find their own?"

"But, I don't want one. Girls suck."

"Watch your mouth, kiddo," Brayden warned, and Cameron blushed.

"Sorry," he whispered.

Abby just smiled, and the rest of lunch went peacefully, despite the tension radiating from Brayden.

When they were finished, Bray stood and picked Lacy up. "Okay, I have you guys for the afternoon. Let's go play some T-ball."

Aiden and Cameron pumped their fists, and Lacy rolled her eyes. Brayden nuzzled her neck, and she giggled.

"Come on, squirt. I need to show you how it's done so we can beat your brothers."

She smiled and kissed Brayden's cheek.

"Okay," she whispered.

Well, dear Lord, Abby was pretty sure one of her ovaries exploded with the cuteness surrounding her. A sexy, alpha man holding a little girl and being all fatherly? Why couldn't she have that?

An image of Tyler flashed in her mind, and she blinked.

Damn, she had to stop thinking about that. He didn't want her, not really. She'd just be a novelty to him. A notch on his bedpost that was sure to have more notches than sense. She'd be okay once she moved.

She would.

Sure, keep telling yourself that.

Allison came up to say goodbye to her kids and nodded at Brayden. Abby couldn't hear what they said, but Bray merely nodded then walked out the door with the kids, leaving a longing Allison behind.

Darn it. It was February, the month of love and relationships. Why was everything so hard? Oh, yeah, because it was only fun for whoever actually had someone, not for those waiting on the perimeter for something to happen.

And she was tired of waiting. It was time to be proactive and move on.

"Want to come in back when I eat my lunch so you can tell me what's going on with you?" Allison asked as she tucked a piece of auburn hair behind her ear. At thirty, Allie looked her age because of lack of sleep and stress, but she was still one of the most beautiful women Abby had ever known.

If only Allie would do something about her loneliness and Brayden.

Yeah, like Abby had anything to say about that, considering she was running away.

No, not running away, just ready to find a new life.

"Sure, I can't go into the kitchen, but I can hang out in the break room, right?" Abby asked as she picked up her coat and purse.

"Yep, I'll be back in a minute. Sally's going to take over, and then I have only a couple hours left in my shift, thank God."

Abby went to the back, but she didn't have to wait long because Allison was there shortly with a club sandwich and a soda.

When she sat down, Allie let out a sigh that Abby was sure she felt in her bones. "Oh, thank God, I'm exhausted. These two-a-days are killing me."

"Isn't there somewhere else you can work?" Abby asked.

Allie gave her a long look, then snorted. "Yeah, in Holiday? For a woman with three kids and a high school education? Um, no, honey, but it's okay. The kids are fed, clothed, and housed. We're alive."

"I just wish there was something I could do."

"You're leaving, Abby; we'll be okay."

"Well, just make me feel worse, why don't you?"

Allie held Abby's hand and squeezed. "I know why you're leaving, and I don't begrudge you for it. Holiday is just too small for people like us, people who don't conform. I can't leave because this is where my children are—this is their home. But, you can leave, Abby. Find your happiness."

Tears filled her eyes, and Abby nodded. "Thanks for understanding."

"That doesn't mean I like it though."

"Oh, I wouldn't think you would. I'm not really happy that I'm leaving my friends, but I need to do this."

"I know, hon. There's nothing for you here, nothing to meet your needs."

"Tyler asked me out," Abby blurted out.

Allie froze then slowly lowered her soda. "Say again?"

"Tyler asked me out on a date or whatever. I went over there to say goodbye because I'm a freaking idiot, and he asked me out." She left out the part about the arrows, not knowing what to say.

"Well then."

"Pretty much."

"What are you going to do about it?"

"Nothing. He's just asking me out because I'm leaving. I'm not in the mood to get my heart broken again, sorry."

Allie nodded, understanding in her eyes. "I'm sorry, hon."

"I'll be okay. I have to be."

Allie didn't say anything else on the subject, and Abby left shortly after, knowing it was one of their last goodbyes. Was she doing the right thing?

God, she hated doubting herself. Damn Tyler. No, she couldn't blame him totally, not when she'd always had doubts. It was still nice to simply place all the issues on him anyway.

The wind howled around her when Abby arrived home, and she cursed. Damn, it looked like another late-season snowstorm was on its way. Just what she needed. She closed the door behind her and turned on the heat, knowing it wouldn't do much good anyway until it kicked on later. Maybe she'd drink some cocoa to warm up. Oh, and maybe eat a few candy hearts—her weakness.

When she got to her kitchen, the hinge on the back door caught her eye. What the heck? It looked as if someone had sawed off part of the hinge and had tried to get through the door. Why would anyone do that?

The hairs on the back of her neck stood

on end, and Abby reached for her heavy-duty rolling pin. Was there someone in the house?

She heard a creak on her floor behind her and turned. Everything went dark, and she hit the floor with a resounding thud.

Chapter 5

Tonight was the night. Tyler would ask out Abigail again, and she'd say yes. There had to be a way. He'd left her alone for the past day so she could get used to the fact that he had changed his tune. Plus, he'd been called into work on his vacation to deal with a last minute paperwork issue.

Damn Mrs. Ellis.

Now he could give Abigail his full attention.

It still hadn't hit him completely yet that he wanted Abigail. He wasn't some school-age boy who wanted something—or someone—only because he couldn't have it anymore. No, that wasn't the case.

It had all happened when he'd touched that arrow. It had felt as if a veil had been lifted...but how? All he knew was that he needed to see Abigail again. To get down on his knees and beg for forgiveness for his shortsightedness. He wasn't the flower-and-chocolates type of guy; he'd do it if she wanted it. But, did she?

Damn, how could he not know?

He'd known her most her life, yet he didn't know if she liked flowers and chocolates or anything like that. He knew she liked candy and other things, but what about for a date? What the hell had happened that he didn't know these things about her? Why was it that he suddenly could *see* her?

He'd spent twenty-four excruciating long hours of waiting for her, formulating his plan, and dealing with the new powers he'd been given. Because of the holiday—*his* holiday—approaching, the pull on his heart was running rampant, and he'd shot more people than he wanted to count in his county, not just in Holiday.

This job was going to kill him. So much for a vacation from his sheriff's position.

He'd followed more couples than he wanted to contemplate, hitting them with arrows so they could see the connection they could share even though sometimes, no, most of the time, a cupid wasn't all powerful, and the couple would resist the connection anyway. Romance and love was a complicated mess, and he was just a part of it.

At least he hadn't had to wear tights. Small favors.

He tucked in his dress shirt then rolled up the cuffs. He looked in the mirror and sighed. He needed a haircut. His usually closely cropped hair was starting to get too long for him, though it still wasn't as long as any of his brothers.

He looked damn old too. He was ten years older than Abigail. Ten freaking years.

There had to be laws against that, right? She might be past the age of consent, but that didn't make it right. Maybe that's why he'd ignored her for so long, even though that lie didn't settle right on his tongue.

It could have been the arrow's fault for making him want to ignore her and all the feelings that ran rampant within him. No, it couldn't be. The arrow, according to what the other cupid had written and what Tyler himself felt, only broke down the barriers and showed a person what could be. It allowed that slight or sometimes not-so-slight connection to be revealed so that someone could take that first step.

Was that what had happened? Was he ready to take that first step?

What about Abigail? What did she feel? Damn it, none of this made sense. Abigail was sweet, innocent, so he'd go for casual. She'd like that, right? Damn why was he acting like a teenager?

Tyler wiped his hands down his jeans— yep, clammy.

He'd been with plenty of women before, yet this was different. He winced at the thought. Damn, he shouldn't have thought of his past. He'd never thought he'd be the person to regret what he'd done. No, he'd gone through life thinking that he'd been okay with himself. He'd purposely never given commitments and had been upfront about everything.

He'd loved women—but had never been *in* love with them. All of the women had known what they were getting into, and he hadn't left a trail of broken hearts in his wake, at least, that's what he thought. What if he'd been wrong?

Tyler had never moved past one-night stands and sweaty nights that he could easily forget. It was a wonder that anyone would want him after that. He'd never been an ass about it, but he surely wasn't considered a saint.

Not like Abigail.

No, she was innocence and purity personified. At least in his mind. And with the way the town talked about her—like they talked about everybody as if it was their right as a small community—Abigail had to be the schoolmarm virgin.

It could have been true for all he knew.

Tyler ran a hand through his hair and tried to think about any dates Abigail might have had and came up empty. What the hell? Was the source of whatever had been blocking him also blocking memories of Abigail, or had she really never had someone in her life? She was young yet—he winced at the reminder—but there had to have been at least someone...right?

Damn, what the hell was wrong with him? He sat down in his armchair and held his head in his hands. Why was he acting like this? He hadn't even asked her out, and yet, he was just going to go over there and expect her to be ready for him. Hadn't she yelled at him on her way out? What if she said no?

Oh, it had occurred to him.

Though he might have been confident with other women when he'd dared to ask them out or when he'd said yes to the outgoing ones who flirted with him, he didn't have a shred of confidence when it came to Abigail.

Tyler knew he wasn't good enough for her, but maybe she'd take him as is.

They were friends after all...right?

The front door opened, and Tyler swung to see the intruder and cursed.

"What the hell, Bray?" Tyler said as he got up and walked to his very unwelcome brother. "What the hell's wrong with you? We don't knock anymore?"

Bray blinked at him, confusion marring his face. "When have we ever knocked? We're Coopers. What's up with you?"

Tyler let out a breath and walked to his bar. Maybe a drink would help his nerves. But, wait; maybe Abigail wouldn't like it if he had liquor on his breath. Damn it. Why was all of this so hard?

"Ty? What's got you so wound up?"

"Abigail," he said without thinking. Well, there went any plan of hiding his newfound feelings. His brothers and Jordan already knew he was a cupid thanks to Brayden's big mouth, so why not let them know he, apparently, had feelings for a woman ten years younger than him who happened to be their best friend?

Oh, yeah, that was the way to do it.

He needed to be smacked or something. Tyler risked a glance at Bray's stunned expression and winced. Maybe his brother would hit him. That might help whatever the hell was wrong with him.

"Abby? The girl you've ignored since puberty? The woman who's been the Coopers' best friend while you've been a complete ass who hasn't even thanked her for all the thankless work she does for you? That Abby?"

Tyler growled, even as shame washed over him. "It's Abigail." He didn't know why that mattered. She went by Abby, but he loved the sound of her name. God, what the hell was wrong with him? He'd been a complete ass to her for as long as he could remember, and now he wanted her. He wasn't a fickle man, but something had happened. Something was wrong.

Bray threw up his hands and scoffed. "Really? That's what you got out of what I just said? Call her whatever name you like—as long as you're not a fucking ass. But, for God's sake, Ty, Abby—sorry, *Abigail*—really? Why does she have you in a tizzy? What could she have possibly done now to anger you? She's fucking moving, Tyler. She says it isn't because of you, but it's not totally *not* because of you."

"I have no idea what you just said."

Bray let out a sigh. "She's leaving

because she feels she has no future here. Ty, you walk all over the girl while she follows you around hoping that you'll notice her. She's grown up now, Ty. She doesn't want to be that person anymore, and I, for one, am happy to hear that. But, you need to let her go. She won't be around to make sure everything you need is taken care of. She won't be around for you to ignore anymore. She's leaving all of us, and you need to get that through your thick skull."

Tyler took a deep breath, even as the thought of never seeing her again ate at him. This feeling, this sense of loss, *this* was real. He hadn't noticed before how every emotion he'd felt toward Abigail before had been muted, dulled. Why the hell hadn't he noticed?

"Something's different now, Bray."

"Yeah, she's leaving, and now you want what you can't have."

Tyler shook his head. "No, I mean something was wrong before. I can't explain it, but it was as if something was blocking me from her before."

Bray raised a brow and sneered. "Really? That's the excuse you're going with?"

"No, hear me out. It's like everything

that had to do with her before had a shield in front of it. But, now...now I can *see* her."

Bray looked at him a long time then let out a breath. "You really believe that?"

"I'm a cupid, remember? I can *feel* these things."

"Okay then, why are you just now feeling them or whatever?" Bray sat down across from him and ran a hand through his hair.

"I accidentally cut myself on my arrow when I was taking it from Abigail."

Brayden sucked in a breath and opened his mouth to speak, but Tyler held his hand to stop him.

"Wait, let me finish. The arrow doesn't make someone fall in love; it's not like that. All it does is show the person holding back what could happen if they let their heart make its own path. I know it sounds odd, but a cupid only helps things along; my powers don't cause love."

"So you're telling me you love Abby."

Tyler shook his head. "No, I mean, I don't know." He closed his eyes and thought of her smile, her curves, and laugh. "I mean I could. I've known her forever, Bray, and I feel like I'm finally sensing my own feelings for the first time in ages. It's like something has been hindering me this whole time. Like I've been falling in love with her since we were both old enough to think we knew what love is, and yet I couldn't feel it. I don't know, Bray, but something was wrong before."

Brayden gave him a hard look and nodded. "So we need to figure out what was blocking you before."

"You believe me?" Hope filled him. If Brayden believed him, then there was a chance Abigail would.

God, he'd hurt her so much with his callous attitude and inattentiveness. Abigail deserved kindness, hope, not someone who shunned her.

Tyler knew he wasn't good enough for her, but maybe he could prove his worth...but how?

"I've never heard you talk like this, Ty. Even if you're confused about what you're feeling, at least you're feeling. Something's up, and we're going to find out what it is, but how?

I don't know what's wrong with this town, but us Coopers sure have to deal with a lot of magical shit, and I'm getting tired of it."

At the sharpness of his tone, Tyler glanced at his brother. There was a haggardness surrounding Brayden that Tyler hadn't noticed before. What magical things were going on with him that Tyler had been too preoccupied to notice?

"Brayden?"

"Let's deal with your problem, okay?" Brayden pleaded.

Tyler nodded, but he knew that wouldn't be the last of it. No, he'd get up off his ass and help Brayden anyway he knew how. But first, he needed to figure out how to get Abigail.

Jesus, his vacation wasn't so much a vacation anymore.

An image of Abigail on a beach wearing nothing but suntan lotion and a smile popped up in his brain, and he held back a groan. Well, that was one way to spend a vacation...

One day...

He shook his head and tried to get his

mind on the task at hand, aware that they were ignoring whatever was going on with Brayden— for now—so they could figure out what to do about Abigail.

Oh, and why he'd ignored her for so long.

Because for the life of him, he couldn't figure out why. Yeah, he hadn't wanted to settle down for a long time, but with Abigail...

Wait. Settle down?

He was just thinking about a date. Maybe a few more after that.

An image of Abigail swollen with his child filtered into his mind, and he froze. Why did that look so appealing when he wasn't ready for a wife and kids? Hence why he'd dated around with no commitments for so long.

Maybe Abigail would change all that.

Tyler clutched his chest and tried to slow his breathing. Apparently, his subconscious had been thinking along the lines of happy and home with Abigail, even when the rest of him had strayed away from those thoughts. That had to be the only explanation for the feelings of rightness when Abigail and his—no, *their*—future came to mind.

"Tyler?" Brayden asked, and Tyler shook his head to clear thoughts that were going way too fast for him.

"Sorry, yes, we'll just deal with my issues now," Tyler finally answered. "But, whatever it is that's bothering you, I hope you know I'll help if you need it."

"I don't know if I like this new caring-brother thing you're doing."

"Hey, I've always been caring, just a bit of an ass at times."

"At times?" Brayden smiled. "Let's get back to the subject at hand, shall we? From what I'm getting, you feel as though something has been blocking you from Abigail all this time."

"Yeah, which sounds crazy."

Brayden shook his head. "No, not in this town. I mean Justin battled Jack Frost over the holidays, so we really don't have any room to talk about crazy. Speaking of Justin, he said something interesting to me about you concerning this before."

"What?" What could Justin know about this?

"I'm not saying he knows what's going on, just that he noticed something going on. He even said the words "blocked" to me over Christmas. So I don't think you're as crazy as you think you are."

"I never said I was crazy," Tyler growled.

Brayden rolled his eyes. "Fine, I put the crazy label on it, but really, if this were last year, I don't think we'd be having this conversation."

"True, but I don't know what the hell is going on, Bray."

"I know, one step at a time, okay? I know you feel like you want Abigail now, but are you sure about that? She's like a sister to me, to all of us Coopers—except you it seems. If you hurt her, we'll kick your ass."

"Good to know brothers stand up for each other, but I see that. If I hurt Abigail—more than I already have—I give you permission to hurt me."

"Do you love her?"

"I...I don't know. It's too soon, and I haven't even kissed her or taken her on a date, but it's like all those feelings that were blocked or whatever the hell it was for so long are back in full force and freaking me the hell out."

Brayden's eyes widened. "Shit. I don't know what happened, Ty, but something will make sense eventually. That said, I think you have one hell of an uphill climb in front of you. She's moving once she sells her home. I think you're lucky because she hasn't signed a new lease in Denver yet because she's waiting for the strings to be cut fully here. Even then, you've ignored her for so long, what's she going to say?"

Tyler smiled at her reaction, even though it hadn't ended well. "I asked her out, and she told me to fuck off."

Brayden threw his head back and laughed. "That doesn't sound like Abby. I like it though. What's your plan?"

Tyler looked down at his hands and shrugged. "I was going to go over tonight and see if she wanted to have dinner with me. I know she'll probably have plans, but I don't want to wait."

"Ballsy, but go for it. Does she know you're a cupid?"

"Damn, I forgot. She saw the arrows, which in itself should tell you something since, apparently, only my true love, or whatever manlier name you want to give it, should be able to see them. But, when I cut myself on it, and asked her out, she kind of forgot about them. But, no, I don't think she knows, not unless Jordan told her."

"She didn't say anything at lunch today, so I'm pretty sure she didn't think of it. It does sound pretty farfetched."

Irrational anger filled him. "You had lunch with Abigail today?"

Brayden cocked his head. "I usually do when I'm watching Ally's kids. Abby loves those kids like her own. She's my friend, Tyler. I'd stop it with the macho jealousy act since she didn't even say she wanted to go out with you tonight."

Tyler let out a breath. "I have no fucking clue what I'm going to do. I mean, what the hell could have put a spell on me? Dear God, did I just say spell? I miss the old days of no magic."

"We never had those. We've always

known what Jordan was, Ty. Okay, that's it. We'll ask Jordan tomorrow and try to figure it out, okay? If she doesn't know, maybe Rina will. She's an elf from the North Pole after all and has lived her whole life without having to hide the magic all around her. They're bound to know something. You're not alone, Tyler."

"I think I'm starting to realize that."

"Good, now I'm going to go home and crash because those kids took all my energy. I don't know how Allison does it."

Tyler smiled. How Brayden didn't know his own feelings toward Allison was beyond him. On second thought, since Tyler hadn't known what he was feeling about Abigail, maybe it was something in the water.

"You're saying three kids knocked the energy out of you? They're like half your size. You're getting old, man," he teased.

"Fuck you. And those kids are energy suckers. Dear Lord, I'm surprised I'm not in a puddle right now. The little one just looks at you with those big puppy-dog eyes and you're a goner."

Yeah, his brother was a goner in more ways than one.

"Whatever you say, man. I'm going over to Abigail's tonight. I want to see her. No, I *have* to see her. I can't believe I wasted all this time."

Brayden frowned. "If something or someone did this to you so you couldn't feel what you needed to then it's something that we'll have to uncover. I'm sorry you lost what you did. But, now you have a chance to move forward and try to show her what you feel. Don't lose that."

If only Brayden could hear his own words and act toward Allison, but Tyler figured there was another story there. One he had no idea of how to fix right now, but hopefully, there'd be time to understand it all.

First though, he had to get Abigail.

Brayden walked out the door, leaving Tyler alone with his thoughts while he tried to get the courage to go over to the home of a woman he wanted, a woman he thought he might love, but who he had just found.

This wasn't love at first sight. No, it felt like something that had molded over time and built on layers of trust and circumstance.

Yet he'd blocked it all away for so long.

How could Abigail even want him now? He thought back to the way he'd treated her for so long and winced. She'd always been there for him, yet he'd taken her for granted. He'd used her up and spat her out because he hadn't seen her.

Well, fuck that.

He'd get down on his knees and beg if he had to because there was no way he'd let her slip though his fingers. He'd do what he could to show her that he was worth it. He just had to prove it.

The doorbell rang, and Tyler frowned. Like Brayden had proven, his brothers would have just walked right in. For a second, he thought it might be Abigail, but he quickly shook off that thought.

She'd already left him once, and he figured she wouldn't be back. Plus he couldn't *feel* her through his new cupid senses, something he'd have to explore further because that scared the hell out of him.

The doorbell rang again, and Tyler cursed. "Coming, hold up."

When he opened it, a tall stranger with dark hair and eyes stood there. He stared at

Tyler with what Tyler was pretty sure was a dark attitude.

"Can I help you?" he asked, for some reason really wishing he had his gun on his belt, rather than locked away in the gun safe.

"No, not really, but I need you anyway," the man said, his words low and deep.

Just who the hell was this guy?

"Who are you?" he asked.

"I see you don't remember me," the other man said as he blinked slowly, almost calculated. Okay, this guy was starting to freak him out.

"No, I don't. What is it you need?" He was done being polite. If the guy didn't say something informative in the next few seconds, he'd slam the door in his face.

"As I said, I need you and your pain. I'm Aeneas, one not of you."

What the hell kind of name was that and what did he mean "one not of you"?

"What?"

Aeneas looked over his shoulder and

smiled. "I'm not a cupid like you, boy. I'm better than that, but this is neither the time nor place to talk about this."

Tyler's heart raced, and his shoulder blades itched where his wings threatened to come out. "How the hell do you know what I am?"

Aeneas shouldered his way into Tyler's home with a strength Tyler hadn't been expecting. "I know more than you think, but that's not why I'm here. No, I want to know what the hell you did to change the curse."

"What the fuck are you talking about?" His hand ached to grab his gun and protect himself, but he didn't have any choice at the moment but to stand and listen. The other guy, whatever the hell he was, was stronger than Tyler, but that didn't make Tyler weak, not by a long shot.

"I'm talking about the fact that, after all this time, you broke through the curse and now you've seen that little dustmop of a woman. What the hell did you do?"

Dustmop of a woman?

He sure as hell shouldn't be talking about Abigail.

"I have no idea what you're talking about."

Aeneas growled and, before Tyler could blink, had his hand wrapped around Tyler's neck and his body against the wall. Tyler clawed at the other man, trying to get free so he could breathe, but Aeneas was stronger.

"Don't lie to me, boy. You cupids are all alike—idiots. Where are your arrows? You know better than to use one on yourself, don't you?"

Tyler gasped for breath, even as his body became light with the lack of air. Fuck, he wasn't the weakest of men, but Aeneas made him feel like a weak kid against him.

"Fuck, you used an arrow, and it counteracted mine. Fuck. Now I'm going to have to take away your love the old-fashioned way, aren't I? Damn you cupids. Why won't you all just fade to ash like the old relics you are?"

What the hell? No, Aeneas couldn't hurt Abigail. He struggled harder, his body twisting as much as it could against the other man or whatever the hell he was.

"I'm not going to kill you now. No, I want you to live with the pain of losing your love like I did. I have the one you want. She's mine for now and you'll have to search hard to find her. Poor Abigail, she had been so close to leaving and never looking back."

Aeneas squeezed harder. Black spots formed in front of Tyler's eyes, and his body went lax.

The last thought that entered his mind as he passed out was of Abigail. Why had he taken so long? He'd save her. He had to.

Chapter 6

Abigail's eyelashes fluttered as she tried to wake up from her nap. For some odd reason, her body felt sore, as though she hadn't slept enough. She stretched her arms over her head, expecting to hit the soft pillows on her bed, and blinked. No, not pillows. No, that was cement.

Cold cement that didn't exist in her own

home.

Where was she?

Wait... she hadn't taken a nap. No, she'd just gotten back to her kitchen, and something had struck her. Then she passed out.

It was all a blur, but clarity was creeping its way back in.

She preferred it as a blur.

Oh, God, this had to be a nightmare. There was no way someone would kidnap her and put her somewhere unknown. No one but the Coopers and a select few even cared about her, so no one would possibly go to these lengths...right?

Oh, God, maybe that's what the killer — *oh please let it not be a killer and just let it be her overactive imagination*—needed. A victim with no hope of friends and family finding her before it was too late because they were too busy worrying about their own lives and problems.

Oh, God, she was going to die.

Abby smacked herself on the forehead and tried to control her breathing. Okay, maybe

Supporting

BritishRedCross

This image on this card was taken at a British Red Cross Open Gardens fundraising event.
To find out about an open garden near you, visit redcross.org.uk/opengardens

recycle

SPRDD14 D/E

yelling out God's name in her head and overreacting wasn't the way for her to be acting at this precise moment. Maybe she'd just passed out and someone had brought her here, wherever *here* was, to make sure she was better.

Yes, Abby, and that unicorn that just passed by has a rainbow coming out of its butt.

Okay, she could do this. She'd read enough romance novels where the heroine got kidnapped and the hero came in and saved the day. Though she liked the other ones better, the ones where the woman actually did something to get herself out of trouble if there was a way.

Yes, she'd do that.

First step, try not to cry like a baby even though the urge seemed insurmountable at the moment.

She was stronger than this.

Where was that sword-wielding woman in the tight black leather that she secretly wanted to be? Not that she even owned leather, but the thought had merit. She refused to be the fainter who swooned under pressure.

Oh, God, was she getting light-headed?

Okay, second step, get control of herself.

Easier said than done.

Third step, get to know her surroundings so she could get out of there. Or at least try. That's what the heroine always did, right?

And they said romance novels never taught anyone anything.

She'd prove them wrong.

And get the heck out of there.

It looked as if she were in an old bunker or unfinished room. The cement walls were old, and she could see the wall cracked in some places. The cold that leached into her bones made it feel as though the heat wasn't on or the building couldn't retain it. There were cobwebs in every corner and the sound of scurrying as something moved away in the distance.

Yep, she wouldn't be thinking about that.

Wow, look how calm she was acting.

Yeah, as long as she ignored the sound of her pulse in her ears as her heart seemed to want to do the mambo. Or was it the samba?

There was one small window that she wouldn't be able to reach unless she scaled the wall, and she didn't think that was going to happen. Plus, she wasn't sure her chest or hips would fit through the small space. Yeah, that would be the last thing she needed. Her body stuck with her butt left in the room for whoever had kidnapped her.

She shuddered at the thought.

Okay, new plan.

There was a door on the other side of the room, but she couldn't tell if it was locked or not until she tried. But then, she didn't know what was on the other side of it either.

She could do this. She'd just find a weapon and open the door and sneak out. Then she'd run for help.

Yes, that sounded like a plan.

In reality, all she wanted to do was hide in a corner, close her eyes, and wait for her body to wake up so she'd find herself at home in her bed, warm and toasty, preferably with Tyler wrapped around her.

Well, if she were dreaming, she might as well go all out, and that sounded like the best plan.

Tyler.

Maybe if someone noticed her missing, he'd come for her. She didn't think *he'd* be the one to notice, but maybe one of his brothers would and tell him. He was the sheriff after all. But who would notice her missing? She'd told everyone she needed some time to pack and get ready to leave. It might be days before anyone noticed.

Oh, God.

She really was all alone.

Like the cat lady without the cats who everyone thought she was to begin with.

Well crap, it looked like she'd have to save herself.

A notion that didn't sit well with her.

Okay, what was next on her list?

Oh, yeah, a weapon. She looked down at herself to see if she had anything on her she could use and froze.

Holy hell, that hadn't been what she'd been wearing when she'd been attacked.

A shudder ran through her as her stomach revolted. She barely held her emotions in and bit her lip so she wouldn't cry.

Someone had changed her. They'd seen her naked and touched her...and who knows what else?

Oh, God.

Why had she thought the first nightmare was the worse? No, it could get so, *so* much worse.

She wore a sensual crimson dress that fell to mid-thigh and hugged her curves. It had a heart neckline that only enhanced her cleavage and made her feel like a vixen.

At any other time, she might have enjoyed looking like a bombshell.

Now?

Abby wanted to throw up.

Why would someone put her in this? She looked down at her stiletto-encased feet and cursed. It had to have been a man. No woman would purposely wear these. She'd have to go barefoot because there was no way she could walk, let alone escape, in them.

Her hair was off her shoulders in an updo thing that surprised her. Who wanted her trussed up like this? Dear Lord, did the kidnapper want her dressed like a date before he killed her?

She really needed to stop reading romantic suspense because now horror stories from authors like Shiloh Walker were on her mind and a little too vivid for what she needed at the moment.

Quickly, she took off her shoes and padded on bare feet to the door on shaky legs. She had to do this. There was no use crying in a corner and wishing for things to be different. Even though that's exactly want she wanted to do.

Abby held her breath and put her ear to the door, straining to hear anything on the other side.

Nothing.

That either meant the door was solid enough that she couldn't hear the scariness on the other side, or she was alone. At least alone enough for her to try and open the door.

She could do this.

There really wasn't another choice. She didn't want to die today—or any day in the near future.

And all of this meant nothing if the door was locked. Steadying herself, she twisted the knob and bit her lip so she wouldn't squeal out in glee when it turned.

Unlocked.

Small favors, right?

She slowly cracked open the door and looked through. There was only an empty hallway that led to another door, dimly lit with a bare bulb.

Okay, could this get any more serial-killeresque?

Abby stepped one barefoot out and then the other. She could do this. Just a few more feet, and she'd be at that other door. Hopefully it would lead to the outdoors so she could run. Where? She had no idea, but it had to be better than this.

She got to about three feet from the door when someone reached out and grabbed her arm.

"Where the hell do you think you're going?" a deep voice asked as she thrashed, trying to get away from him.

Her heartbeat sped up, and tears filled her eyes.

Damn it.

She'd been so close. So freaking close.

The man pulled her back into the room and threw her to the ground. Pain ricocheted up her side when she landed funny, and she scurried back to the wall so she could put distance between her and the man who'd fill her nightmares for years to come.

That is, if she even *had* years to come.

"Who...who are you?" she asked, her voice a little too shaky for her own good.

Her dress had ridden up so she was sure she was flashing the guy, and she tried to pull it down. She needed at least some dignity—even if it seemed false in every way possible.

The man looked down at her with his dark eyes and brushed his even darker hair away from his face. If he hadn't had the expression of someone who was about to kill her, she may have even said he was handsome with those strong cheekbones and masculine jaw. But, the feeling of death seeping off of him and that tired fallen-from-grace look didn't appeal to her.

No, the hunky sheriff who probably hadn't even known she'd gone missing was what appealed to her.

Good going, Abigail.

"My name is Aeneas," the man finally answered. He said it so quickly that it rolled off his tongue as if he'd spoken in an ancient language.

Very, very odd.

Great, now she knew his name. But, how did that help her?

"I regret I had to take you like that, but plans had changed, so I had to make sure you were easy and reliable," he said as he turned his back to her to close—and lock—the door, trapping himself inside with her.

Or should that be, *her* trapped with *him*?

"What are you talking about?" she

asked. The man made no sense. But really, should a killer-kidnapper, or whatever the hell he was, make sense?

Why couldn't she just be at home packing to leave?

"Ah, I see I've started from the middle when you've probably wanted me to start from the beginning. But, you see, that would take far too long for what I have planned for you."

Planned?

Oh, God, that didn't sound good. Not in any sense of the word.

"I see the fear in your eyes, Abigail. But, fear not, I'm not going to kill you."

Relief spread through her for an instant before the foreboding crept in with the spindly tendrils of awareness.

There were things worse than being killed.

Far worse.

"I'm not going to rape you either," he said, even as he tucked a piece of hair behind her ear that had fallen from the chignon he'd fashioned for her.

"Good to know," she blurted out, and she slapped a hand over her mouth.

Great, antagonize the crazy man. Wasn't that rule number seven or something of things not to do when kidnapped by an insane person? Or maybe it was number one. Whatever number it was, it ranked right up there with not running up the stairs from the crazy knife-wielding killer, and Abby wasn't doing so well at the moment.

Aeneas smiled, showing his full set of very white teeth. Though they didn't look like sharp fangs, she could just imagine them morphing into those before devouring her flesh.

Oh, that's just great. Add another nightmare onto the living one she couldn't escape from.

"Good for you. You should say what's on your mind, darling. Hiding from yourself, as well as the town, for so long didn't really do anything for you, did it? I mean, all those toys you have in your nightstand drawer were for naught, weren't they?"

Abby's eyes widened, and she swallowed the bile that had risen in her throat.

Oh, God, how long had this man been watching her? And why did he know those intimate details of her life? No one knew, only her.

He'd said he wouldn't rape her...but, what else did he have planned?

"I see I've surprised you. I think you need to know the whole story. But, first, I need to make sure you don't get the idea to run away again." He took out handcuffs from his back pocket and smiled. "Let me see your hands, darling."

Abby hid them behind her back. There was no way she'd let him handcuff her to anything.

No freaking way.

Aeneas glared. "Stupid bitch. You really think you have any choice in the matter? I was being nice to you because I didn't feel like fileting your body in the delicious way it could be. Believe me, all those curves would lead to a masterpiece of precision cuts. Now give me your fucking hands before you make me lose my temper."

Fear wound its way up her spine and threatened to choke her. Jesus, this wasn't a man to mess with, no matter how nice he tried to smile and console her.

Shakily, she held out her arms, putting her wrists together so he could easily cuff them. He snapped one in place around her right wrist, tugged, and brought her hands above her head to secure her other wrist so that her hands were wrapped around the radiator.

Her pulse sped up as he traced a finger down her jaw.

"I'm sorry to have to do this, like I said, but plans changed."

"What...what plans?"

Keep him talking.

That's all she had to do and maybe someone would come for her. Damn it, she hated being weak.

"Ah, you see, I'm Aeneas. *The* Aeneas."

She blinked. That didn't mean anything to her.

Aeneas—*the* Aeneas, whatever the hell that meant—gave a drawn-out sigh and threw his hands up.

"You damn Americans. How do you know nothing of your history? I'm Aeneas, the first put-upon man and victim of Cupid."

Abby blinked again. Of all the strange things she'd heard in her life, that had been the craziest. And considering she was best friends with a witch and an elf, that was saying something.

"Cupid? Like *the* Cupid?" she asked, the fear of him staunching any humor that may have wanted to wind its way through her voice.

"Yes, the original Cupid. You know of Santa and his executives, well, Cupid has his own, but rather than call them something else, the narcissistic bastard just calls them cupids—little c."

Where on earth was this going?

"I was Cupid's first victim. He used me and...*her* to see if his arrows would work."

"And did they?" she asked, curious as to why he wouldn't say her name. The emotion he said it with lay heavily on him. She wouldn't ask for the woman's identity. Considering how he had her chained, it didn't seem like a good idea to bring that up.

"At first." He closed his mouth, as if sorry he'd said anything at all, even as his eyes stormed over.

"I'm sorry," she said. Even though she didn't know the whole story, something bad must have happened to turn him this way.

Okay, now she was getting sympathetic for the man who had her cuffed. She needed therapy.

A lot of therapy.

Aeneas nodded then pulled something out of his back pocket.

Those tears that had finally stopped running came back in full force as she looked at the length of the blade in his hands.

"I...I thought you said you weren't going to kill me."

"I'm not, Abigail. No, I'm going to show that cupid of yours what it means to ruin my plans."

Her body shook as he came near. She kicked out, but he grabbed her ankle.

"Don't even think about it."

She pulled back, even as he came closer with the knife.

Something he'd said finally snagged on her brain. "Who are you talking about? Who's my cupid?"

Aeneas gave her a truly baffled look. "Tyler, of course. He's a cupid, one made to find the true loves out in the world and bring them together."

Tyler was a cupid? Why hadn't she known?

Wait, those arrows. Now it made sense. But, what did that have to do with her?

"You see, I hate cupids. They're fucking abominations. Because of them and the man who created them, I lost everything. Well, since I can't have her, other cupids can't have the ones they love."

He thought Tyler loved her? No, that couldn't be further from the truth. The man didn't even look at her. Well, other than earlier when he'd asked her out after cutting himself on the arrow...

Oh, shit.

Aeneas slowly dragged the tip of the blade along her collarbone. She shuddered but didn't move. No, he would hurt her more if she did because of the edge being so close to her neck.

Tears streamed down her face, even as she tried to be strong. He'd said he wouldn't kill her, only wanted to show Tyler what it meant to change plans.

But, what plans?

She had to keep him talking.

"What plans?" she whispered, her voice choked.

"You see each cupid has a soul mate. It's easy for me to find them since I'm an immortal, shunned by Cupid. The old bastard shouldn't have done what he did." Aeneas glared as if he'd thought of whatever Cupid had done, and the knife pressed harder into her skin.

The pain flared as the blade cut through her skin, the warm droplets of her own blood forming their own tears down her chest.

It hurts, oh, God, it hurts.

"You know, blood is of the heart. A true

Cupid in that respect. Not anything like the bastard and his progeny."

He cut again. And again. And again.

Each time, the pain flared, and then she blocked it out. She had to. She'd live, he promised, but how?

The blood seeped into the dress he'd put on her and pooled on the floor. Her body shook, but she hadn't lost that much blood. Not yet.

When he finished, he pulled back and wiped the blade clean on her dress. Fiery pain raged through her as the cuts pulled with each breath.

"You need to see, Abigail. Your blood will show the cupids that they can't win."

The man, or immortal, or whatever the hell he claimed to be, was crazy.

He drew back and walked to the corner and pulled something out she hadn't seen him place there before.

An arrow.

But, not like Tyler's.

No, these were black with crimson-red tips.

"You're a cupid?" she asked, her words slurred with pain.

"No, never. Mine don't show you your true love. No, they take away the one thing that makes you...you. With each cupid, I hit them when they least expect it, and I take away the ability for them to see their own true love. They go through life ignoring them until eventually they lose them altogether. It should have worked, but then you cut Tyler with his own arrow, negating my magic."

He traced a finger along the outside of one of her cuts, and she screamed out in pain.

"You made me so angry, Abigail. Now I have to punish the both of you. When I hit you with this arrow, you won't lose Tyler. No, that's not the thing that makes you...you. I'll take away your kindness...your sweetness. Tyler won't want you when you're a harpy."

"A...harpy?"

"Yes, I can see the beauty in you, and I'll take that and drain it from you. You'll live as a harpy for the rest of your years, and Tyler will want nothing to do with you. You'll both go through life alone and in pain. Something all cupids deserve."

She didn't even know what a harpy was beyond what she'd read in some novels. He couldn't really do it...could he?

Aeneas walked back and pulled out his bow, put the arrow in its place, and shot.

The arrow didn't hurt...no, that wasn't it.

But as the magic spread through her, ripping away something she hadn't known she cherished, she screamed.

Agony, sweet, sweet agony seared her.

And she was lost.

Chapter 7

Something was ringing, but Tyler couldn't shut it off. He blindly reached out to try to turn it off but came up with only air. Hell, he'd have to open his eyes se he could find the damn thing. His eyelids were heavy, as if he'd had a long sleep that didn't equate into the same amount of energy. With as much fight as he could muster, he opened his eyes and cursed.

How the hell had he fallen asleep in his living room on the floor? Make that the *very* hardwood floor. He shifted and groaned at the aches in his not-too-young body. He hadn't done that since college when he'd drunk too much whiskey, trying to beat his brothers. That hadn't turned out too well for any of them. None of them drank whiskey anymore, and Jackson still paled at the thought of it.

Tyler didn't exactly remember drinking, so that couldn't be it.

He swallowed hard, trying to wake up, and winced. Fuck, why did his throat hurt?

Then it came to him.

"Abigail," he croaked out, his throat too sore to do anything else.

Damn it, that man, Aeneas. He'd choked the hell out of him, forcing Tyler to pass out. And the bastard had Abigail. There was no telling what Aeneas would be doing...

Or...what if Tyler was too late?

No, he couldn't think like that. Aeneas

wouldn't have told him about Abigail if there hadn't been a chance he could save her.

Right?

Aeneas had said he'd taken Abigail so Tyler couldn't have his true love...but that couldn't mean it was the end.

It couldn't.

If Aeneas hurt her because of him, he'd never forgive himself. She'd done nothing but exist and become the one he could finally see.

Tyler staggered to his feet and cursed. It wasn't time for him to have a fucking pity party when his girl was out there, maybe in pain...maybe worse.

His girl.

As much as he liked the sound of that, he needed to worry about other things. Like where the hell Aeneas had her and how Tyler was going to get her back.

That emotion he'd been hiding or missing or whatever for too long welled up in him and almost made him fall to his knees with the force of the blow.

Goddamn, he loved that woman. Her

smile, her kindness, the way she put everyone first, the way he'd always felt like a better person around her but hadn't even realized it.

He'd kill Aeneas for what he'd done.

Tyler and Abigail had lost so much time because of a curse Aeneas had put on him. But no longer. Tyler would find her and take care of what he had to.

Then he'd have to convince Abigail that it was the curse that had made him act like an ass, not himself, even though, in reality, he was an ass most of the time even without a curse or whatever the hell it was that had stopped him from seeing her...

In fact, he didn't remember much about Abigail and his feelings since he'd gotten home from putting a bandaid on her knee when she'd fallen. And then everything went blurry.

Fuck, magic complicated everything.

Tyler went to his safe, pulled out his gun, and made sure it was loaded but also that the safety was still on. He wouldn't be acting like the sheriff today. No, he'd be on his own. There was no way to explain the magic of Holiday to the others without explaining so much more. There were no exact protocols as to what to do if someone with magic came into town and tried to hurt or kill those they loved.

The Coopers had learned that the hard way with Jack Frost over Christmas when he'd tried to hurt the town, and then specifically Rina and Justin. The two had used their own magic to stop him, but Tyler didn't have that. He had only the ability to find a connection between two people...and his gun.

So he'd use what he needed and then damn the consequences.

They'd have to find a way to police this in the future, but at the moment, all Tyler wanted was to save Abigail.

His Abigail.

Tyler shook his head, trying to clear out the cobwebs that came from being forced to take a nap at the hands of a not-so-good guy and froze. Fuck, that ringing was still going on.

And it was the alarm clock in his bedroom, meaning he'd been unconscious throughout the night.

Fuck.

He walked to his room and slammed his

hand against the clock, cutting of the annoying ringing.

Dear God. How long had Aeneas had her now? It had to have been more than twelve hours. He forcefully swallowed the bile that had risen in his throat. There was no telling what a man—or whatever the hell Aeneas was— could do to an innocent like Abigail in that time frame.

Fuck, no matter what, he'd make her okay; he'd help her.

It was the least he could do.

Tyler needed to find a way to get to her. He pulled on his brown leather jacket so he could at least stay warm, grabbed the first aid kit, and went to his car.

Okay, now how would he find her?

He had no idea where Aeneas was, and he was pretty sure she wasn't at her home considering the bastard had said he'd taken her. But from where? Maybe he should start at her home and work from there. There had to be a trail or something that could lead to her.

Fuck, he couldn't do this alone, could he?

Tyler started his SUV and began the short drive to Abigail's home while calling his brothers—something he knew was damn dangerous but he did anyway.

Matt's voicemail picked up, and Tyler cursed. Fuck, okay, Justin then. When Justin, Brayden, then Jackson's voicemails picked up one right after another, Tyler slammed his hand down on the steering wheel then parked in front of Abigail's home.

How the hell were *all* his brothers busy? It was still early in the morning, but he'd thought at least *one* of them would answer his phone.

Hell, he was all alone in this, and he had no idea what to fucking do.

Damn it. He was the sheriff. He knew how to track and catch the bad guy; it was his job.

His hands shook as he turned off the car and took a deep breath. This wasn't just his job. This was Abigail. The girl—no, woman—who'd been by his side and had helped him with every town function and other thing she could.

Because she was just that good a person.

And, if he were honest, because she had a crush on him.

Fuck, he'd lost so much time because of Aeneas.

Tyler growled and walked toward Abigail's home, a new sense of purpose settling in. He'd find the fucker and take care of him. Abigail would be his, even if he had to get on his knees and beg.

It'd be worth it.

The front door looked to be locked, so he went around to the back, careful to look as though he was just checking in on things in case the neighbors were watching. Damn small town.

When he reached the back, he cursed again. The screen door was off its hinges. Sweat ran down his spine as fear clawed his stomach. Damn it, he knew she'd been kidnapped. Why did seeing this make it more real to him?

He got in the house and didn't see anything out of place. It looked as if she'd set down her purse, and then that was it.

He couldn't see anything else.

She just wasn't there.

How the hell was he supposed to find her?

Tyler rubbed his chest above his heart then froze.

He was a cupid. How the hell had he forgotten that? He already knew that he had a connection with Abigail. He'd felt it the moment he'd cut his finger on the arrow. He now had a cord wrapped around his heart that led to Abigail, like a branch tethering him to the woman he loved.

Fuck, now he was waxing poetry, but he got it.

He just had to follow the cord, the connection, to Abigail.

Now, how the hell did he do that?

He closed his eyes and thought of that connection, the warmth he felt with Abigail. God, how could he have ignored it for so long? He didn't have time to think of the ramifications or exactly what he was going to do about it once he found her and everything had settled. No, that would be for another time.

He needed to find her first.

Their connection was warm like honey, new and fresh, but settled, like it had always been there. He just hadn't seen it. It wrapped around not only his heart but every part of his being, as though it had a place and a right to be there.

He went back to his car and followed that feeling in his heart. The cord continued on to the woods behind her house, miles away and to a place he'd never been before.

He drove along the off-road path and followed the connection. She'd be okay; she had to be. Considering he could still feel her on the other end because of his cupid abilities, that had to mean she was still alive.

Fuck, he didn't even want to think about what state she could be in though.

Maybe Aeneas only wanted to hide her from Tyler.

The other man had said something along the lines of taking her away, it could have meant anything.

Abigail would be okay.

She had to be.

He parked the SUV near a small cement building in the middle of nowhere. It looked like it had once been a supply cabin that had been refitted for the Montana winters before it had been abandoned.

Abigail was alive somewhere in there.

Tyler just had to find a way to get her out.

He slid his fingers against the gun on his hip, and a calm surrounded him. He could do this. For Abigail, he would do anything.

He'd have to think about that thought later.

"It's about time you got here, Tyler. I expected better of you," Aeneas said from the doorway.

Tyler aimed at the bastard but kept his cool. "Where's Abigail?"

"Inside. I didn't kill her. I'd promised her that I wouldn't. Though, to be honest, at this point, she probably wishes she were dead."

Tyler growled but stayed where he was. "So why are you just standing out here? Trying to taunt me? I don't get it. What the hell do you want?"

Aeneas threw his head back and laughed. "What do I want? I want it all back. But I can't have that, can I? No, I'm relegated to roam the earth alone because of that damn Cupid. Now the bastard is up in his god land delegating his duties to the cupids like you, and I'm forced to watch."

"Just who the hell are you?"

"Research your own fucking history if you want to know who I am. I lost everything because of Cupid, and now you're going to lose everything."

Tyler clenched his jaw. "You can't have her."

"Took you long enough to realize that you wanted her in the first place. I was surprised to see how much you love the girl, Tyler. You're the notorious ladies' man and now look at you. Whipped at just the *thought* of having a piece of that virgin pie."

"Shut the fuck up about Abigail."

"Nice mouth you have there. But really, you aren't the saint you need to be for her. Or, would have had to be before I got ahold of her."

Tyler saw red, his body shaking on adrenaline and anger. "What the fuck did you do to her?" He barely, just barely, held himself back so he wouldn't attack the man. Tyler knew he wasn't as strong as Aeneas and needed to take another approach with him.

But, fuck, what had Aeneas done to Abigail?

"I didn't rape her, if that's what you're thinking. She's still as pure as snow for you. That is if you want her once you see her."

"What the fuck did you do?" he repeated, even as the slight relief that Abigail hadn't been harmed in that way filled him.

Would she ever forgive him for the curse and what had been done to her?

Tyler didn't think she should have to.

"I did only the same thing I did to you. I took away the one thing that made her Abigail."

Tyler swallowed hard, not knowing what that could be since everything about her made her unique.

"Now, do you want to see her? Or are

you too scared to see what she's become?"

"I'm going to kill you. Soon."

Aeneas shook his head. "No, you aren't. You're going to try, but in reality, you're going to live alone, without Abigail, because that's who you are. And what you deserve."

Before Tyler could blink, Aeneas knocked the gun out of his hand and had him pinned to the wall.

"You think you're strong, but you're nothing. You're just a fucking cupid."

Tyler struggled against Aeneas's hold, his fists going out and catching Aeneas in the ribs. "I'm not a fucking weakling," he rasped out, and the arm on his throat pressed harder.

"No, you're less than that."

Rage built up within him, and he lashed out. A strength he hadn't known he possessed filled him as he pushed Aeneas back. The other man looked surprised for a moment, and Tyler used that to his advantage. He punched the bastard in the throat then added another hook to his ribs.

Aeneas staggered for a moment then

lashed out, his eyes narrowed and a grimace on his face.

Tyler blocked the next move but got a fist in his stomach instead. He bent over at the waist, coughing and gasping for breath. He lunged at the fucker, bringing him down to the ground, punching with each exhale.

Aeneas pushed back and spit out blood.

"I see you've found your strength as a cupid. Well, fucker, while you're out here playing in the dirt with me, your Abigail is in there, writhing in pain. Is that what you wanted?"

Tyler clenched his fists, ignoring the pain in his side and throat. "What did you do?"

"I shot her with my own arrow. I already told you it takes away the thing that makes her Abigail. Well, your Abigail isn't human anymore. She's a harpy. Something you could never want. So you see, you've still lost. You won't have the one you want, and you'll die alone. Like you should."

"You're wrong," he said even as his mind whirled. A harpy? He shouldn't have been surprised those were real. There were a host of supernaturals out there that they didn't know about.

But a harpy?

How would Abigail react to that?

"We'll see. Now, I'm leaving you to take care of her or ditch her. I really don't care anymore. My work is done, cupid. Don't fuck with me again."

With that Aeneas walked off. Though Tyler desperately wanted to follow him and end the bastard, Abigail was just inside the building, waiting for him or someone to help her.

He ran through the door and followed the connection to her to a back room. When he opened that door, he froze.

Oh sweet Jesus. What had Aeneas done to her?

Cuts marred her body, though they didn't look to be bleeding anymore. She wore a red dress that she'd never have chosen herself. And worse, she lay on the ground, her eyes closed, her mouth open on a moan, and her body writhing on the floor.

She looked human, but in pain.

He quickly ran to her side and knelt by her.

"Abigail, baby. I'm here," he whispered even as his eyes filled.

Fuck.

"Tyler?" she whispered as she opened her eyes.

He brushed some hair out of her face and lowered his lips to her brow. He'd never tasted her skin before, never felt the softness beneath his lips.

God, he loved this woman.

"It's going to be okay, baby. I'll take care of you."

"He shot me with an arrow," she said as she winced in pain.

"I know, Abigail. But I'll take care of you."

She shook her head and moaned. "No, you can't." Her arm lashed out, her fingers stretched into a claw, but he caught her hand and kissed her palm.

"I don't care what he did to you. I'll take

care of you."

"I don't understand."

Neither did he, not really. "It doesn't matter. Let me get my jacket on you, and I'll take you home."

"No, not home. He was in there."

"Then I'll take you to my home." Though Aeneas had been there as well, they'd deal with that later.

"I don't know what's happening to me."

"He told me part of it, but we'll talk about it all later. Together."

She bit her lip but nodded and tried to stand. Quickly, he wrapped his coat around her shoulders and lifted her into his arms. She as so small, so fragile.

He'd fucking kill the bastard for hurting her.

Abigail rested her head on his shoulder and sighed. "I don't know what's happening to me, but I don't think it's good."

"We'll figure it out," he repeated. Her body was warm, too warm, and he knew he'd have to make real plans once they got back to his place.

"I trust you, Tyler," she whispered as she passed out in his arms.

Warmth spread through him at the thought.

He hoped he earned that trust.

Aeneas had underestimated him and the connection he shared with Abigail. Because no matter what she turned into, Tyler would want her. He just had to prove it to her.

Chapter 8

Abby felt as though she were on fire. The flames licked up her arms, down her back, digging into her flesh and searing her from the inside out. She couldn't open her eyes, couldn't speak—she could only succumb to the flames. Oh, God, the heat. It wasn't a normal heat where she could run away and cool off. No, this one started in her belly and spread like the wildfire it was.

She had to be dying.

Or...what had Aeneas said?

She felt the sweat roll down her temples, her spine, and everywhere else as she rocked back and forth in the chair...or was she on the floor? She wasn't sure anymore.

What was happening? What was she turning into?

A harpy.

Abby didn't know what that was beyond the crazy demon-like creatures she'd read about in some of her romance books. She moaned as the pain flared, trying to suck her into the abyss. She knew if she fell, she wouldn't be able to climb her way out. No, she had to focus on something else.

What did she remember about harpies?

They had claws—sharp talons that could tear through flesh as if it were butter. They were warriors. Some stories even said they were stronger than any other supernatural creature in the world, or any world for that matter.

That was, of course, if she believed in such things.

She didn't know what to believe anymore.

Some stories said they had wings, their only weakness.

The sharp pain stabbed at her again, and she gasped. Oh, God, thinking wasn't working.

"Abigail, baby, open your eyes and look at me. Breathe, baby," a voice said as it wrapped around her like velvet.

Her body cooled from the pain but warmed from a whole new sensation at the thought.

Why did that voice sound so familiar?

"Abigail, open your eyes. We're home now; you're safe. I'll take care of you, baby, but you need to open your eyes. I need to know you're okay." Desperation laced his tone, along with something else, something that sounded like care or...love.

Who was it?

No one loved her. Not like that.

A vision of Tyler's face filled her mind, and she sighed, the pain not so bad anymore. It was only her wish that the voice belonged to him. It couldn't be his...could it?

Her rescue came back to her, and she gasped. Tyler had come for her. He'd gotten her out of that room, had held her to his chest and cradled her like something precious.

Could the voice belong to him?

Abby forced open her eyes, the slow movement tearing at her, but she needed to see. Needed to feel something other than pain.

"Tyler?" she croaked out, and the man in front of her smiled.

It was him. Tyler, the man she loved and the man Aeneas said she'd never have. His strong jaw and cheekbones were fixed in a state of tension, even through his smile. His blue eyes were a deep pool of ocean water framed by dark lashes. His hair was a dark brown, short, cut close to his head.

That whole military-cop look was always sexy on him.

And he'd called her baby.

Maybe she was still dreaming.

"Hey, Abigail, it's me," Tyler said as he traced her jaw with his finger then pushed the hair from her face. "How are you feeling?"

"Hot," she said then blushed. Well, yeah, she was hot for something, but it wasn't the fact that her body was on fire.

Oh great, way to look desperate.

Tyler brought a cool cloth to her face and neck, touching her so gently she wanted to weep.

"What happened?" she asked.

Tyler's face stormed over, but he kept his touch gentle. "Aeneas took you from your home, but you're safe now. I'll take care of you."

She looked at her surroundings and sighed. He'd brought her to his home, not hers. She'd vaguely remembered asking him not to bring her home. She hadn't wanted to be at the place where Aeneas has taken her. The final pieces of where she'd been and what had happened slipped into place, and she looked down at her body, expecting to see the pools of blood and cuts from the non-cupid maniac that had smiled when he'd cut into her flesh.

But now she saw only long, healed scars.

"How long have I been asleep?"

"Only an hour or so, baby."

"But, no, that doesn't make sense. How can I be healed like this?"

Tyler pressed the cool cloth to her temple and gave her a sympathetic look. She wasn't going to like his answer.

Her body bent in pain and her hands felt as though someone had sliced into them. She cried out and looked at her fingers.

"Oh, God, Ty," she whispered.

In place of her hands were claws with long, pointed nails that looked like they could rip a heart of out of someone's chest with one swipe.

No, this couldn't be happening. She didn't want to be a harpy. Harpies were mean, evil, and could only be controlled by the person they loved the most.

This couldn't be her.

"Abigail, it's okay. It'll go away. You're still you."

She shook her head, unbelieving. He picked up her clawed hands and kissed them, sending a coolness through the fiery pain and her claws receded.

"See? I told you it'd be okay."

Tyler had made them go away, not her. What did that mean?

"What do you remember about what happened to you?" he asked, changing the subject.

"I remember everything, Tyler. The way he took me from my home, how he explained that he hated Cupid and all the other cupids—including you." She raised a brow; yeah, they would get to that. "I remember him cutting me then..." She took a deep breath. "Then he hit me with his own arrow. He said it would take away what mattered most about me—my kindness."

Tyler brushed another lock of hair from her face. "He said he'd turned you into a harpy, Abigail. I think that's why you've healed so much and why we just saw your claws."

"But I don't want to be a harpy."

Real mature, but honestly, she didn't know what else to say. Why couldn't she just wake up from this nightmare?

"I know, baby, but we'll take care of it. We'll take it one step at a time together, okay?"

"Why do you keep calling me baby? I thought you didn't even like me." And there was the crux of the matter. She didn't recognize this caring Tyler, though she'd seen him like this with his family. He was a kind man to others, just not her. That's why she hated herself for loving him for so long.

Tyler took a deep breath and ran his hand down her arm to grasp her hand. She didn't pull away, though she should have. She liked the touch of his skin, the calloused fingers on her soft ones. She might have been a glutton for punishment when it came to him, but she was too sick to deal with it. At least that's what she'd tell herself now.

God, she was pathetic.

"Aeneas shot me with an arrow. I don't know when, but it had to be when I was a lot younger. His arrows take away the things that make us ourselves. With you, it took away your kindness, though I don't think he could ever do that, not really. I haven't seen any evidence that you aren't the best Abigail you can be. Yes, you had claws for a moment, but we'll find out what else happens.

"But, with me, it took away my ability to see the one person who would be perfect for me. I'm a cupid. I'm the one who helps people find those who could love each other in each possible and precious way. It makes sense that the one thing that made me myself would be the ability to find my own love."

Memories of every time he'd ignored her or acted like she didn't exist assaulted her. "You're saying it was his arrow that caused you to ignore me and treat me like crap? Because I don't know if I believe that."

Tyler frowned and took a deep breath. "I need you to, Abigail. God, I can't believe I lost so much time. That *we* lost so much time. I didn't see you, not really. You were always there in my peripheral vision. I think deep down I knew who you were...what we could become. I fell in love with you, Abigail, yet, I didn't know it. I *couldn't* know it."

Love? Did he just say love? Because that didn't make sense. People just didn't magically fall in love like that. Not in reality, anyway.

"I can see by the expression on your face you don't believe me. I'll prove it to you, baby. I promise."

"This is really fast, Tyler." Though even as she said it, the woman inside her that loved the man in front of her did a little dance, shaking her hips with glee.

Subtle.

Though the woman inside her wasn't as perky as she usually was, no she seemed a little more sultry. Like a vixen.

"I know. I don't know why I'm not freaking out more than I am either, but we can deal with this, you know. I'm more worried right now that you're in pain. What can I do?"

As he spoke, she felt the pain recede. For some reason, she knew the change was complete, though as she looked down at her body, she couldn't see a change. Maybe it was only on the inside. That didn't sit quite well with her, though. She didn't want to change. She didn't want to lose Abigail.

"I'm okay now, at least I think so. I don't look different, do I? Besides the claws, of course."

Tyler traced a finger along her chin, her lips. Shivers of need scaled over her body as she looked into his eyes to see his pupils dilating.

"You look like Abigail. Beautiful."

She swallowed hard at his words. "This is so weird. I'm not used to you saying things like this to me." Though she loved it.

Tyler nodded but kept touching her. "I know, but I'll fix that. I don't plan on going anywhere."

"What do you mean?"

"I mean now that I've found you, I'm not letting you go. You're stuck with me, Abigail Clarke."

Stuck with Tyler Cooper? Well, that didn't sound too bad. No, not at all.

"What does that mean?"

"It means that I'm going to prove to you that I'm not the same man I was before you cut me with that arrow."

"Wait, it was my fault?"

Tyler laughed, a deep chuckle that reached her in all the right spots. "No, I'm saying that the arrow I cut myself on broke the curse."

"Do you think it could help me?" She tamped down on the hope that swelled. It wouldn't be that easy; she knew it.

Tyler gave a sad smile. "No, baby, I don't think so. My arrows are to help in crumbling the walls people build between themselves and those they could love. That's what happened when I saw you. I love you, Abigail. I can't explain it, but I do. I know it's too fast, so we're going to start fresh."

He loved her.

Maybe she was still dreaming.

"Fresh?"

"Fresh. We're going to start as though we're just now finding each other. I know we have history, and you shouldn't forgive me for the way I've acted, but I want to make it up to you."

"But, you're saying it was because of the

curse."

"I'm saying that a lot of my actions were because of it. But I can't be sure which ones. I mean I was a horrible person to you, Abigail. I ignored you, and I took advantage of your kindness because I didn't think you were really there, not for anything more than just a background. I don't deserve your forgiveness, but I'm going to prove how much I want it. And I'm going to help you deal with whatever being a harpy means. I'm not letting you go."

Cautiously, she lifted her hand to cup his cheek. "I believe you, Tyler Cooper."

He smiled and leaned into her touch. Okay, she was really liking this new Tyler, even though she'd loved the old one, too.

"I don't know what the future brings, Abigail. I'm a freaking cupid, and it's almost Valentine's Day. I'm going crazy enough. But when Aeneas took you..." He shuddered and placed his palm on the top of her hand. "I felt as though I'd lost something I hadn't even realized I had. That bastard is sick, baby. I still don't know why exactly he hates the cupids."

"He said it was because Cupid had taken something away from him. But I don't know what. Maybe there's something we can look up. Cupid was a legend or god or whatever, right?"

"It depends on the mythology, but yeah. I haven't really looked into what being a cupid meant, even though I should have. I've been hiding what it meant to be one this whole time."

"So, you've known what you were for a while then?"

"I've known since I was a kid, but I haven't had to deal with the whole cupid thing until now. This was the first year I've had the arrows and had to deal with the physical connection I feel when I see someone who could love another. I'm still so new to it, and it's kind of weird."

Abby smiled. "So, you shoot people with arrows, sheriff?"

Tyler grinned. "Yes, though they can't see them. I'm still trying not to look like an idiot hiding behind a bush or something so people can't see me playing with thin air."

Abby laughed, the warm feeling spreading through her. She'd be okay; she'd figure it out. Plus, she had Tyler by her side now to help. Well, for as long as he wanted her.

She couldn't get rid of the feeling that, even if it weren't a dream, he'd find someone better. There were so many women who wanted him, and she was "just Abby."

"Hey, what's that look for?"

"Nothing," she lied.

"Are you still doubting me?"

"How can you read my mind? Is it a cupid thing?"

"No, it's a me thing." He cupped her cheek. "I know you don't have any reason to believe me, and I know it's my fault, but I'll prove it to you. I don't want anyone else, Abby."

He leaned down and brushed his lips across hers. He tasted of coffee and candy, sweet and goodness. His lips were firm, yet soft, sinful.

Oh, my God, I'm kissing Tyler Cooper.

Yes! The want-to-be cheerleader in her was shaking her pom-poms and squealing.

She opened her lips and let his tongue dance with hers. She moaned into him, and he pulled back, his gaze heated.

"I've wanted to do that forever, though I didn't know it."

She nodded, unable to speak.

"I'm going to do it again soon. Just warning you," he said as he brushed his thumb along her cheek.

She swallowed hard, trying not to think about that because her body was heated enough. "So, do you wear tights when you're on your cupid adventures?"

Tyler threw his head back and laughed. "Hell, no. Thankfully, we don't have a uniform. Just the arrows, bows, and quiver."

"I would have paid to see that," she teased.

Tyler shook then shifted so he could lie on the couch, bringing Abby with him. She leaned into his hold and inhaled that crisp scent that was just Tyler.

"Sorry to move you. I just wanted to hold you. Okay?"

Hell, yeah, it was better than okay, but she wasn't about to tell him that. She merely nodded while leaning harder into him.

She turned in his arms and he gasped.

"What?"

"Let me check your back, okay, baby?"

Fear slid through her. "Why?"

"I just need to check something," he said, his voice calm.

She turned in his arms and let him pull up her shirt slightly. She blushed at the thought of what he would be seeing even as nervousness ate at her.

"Well, that's new," he whispered.

"What? Oh, my God. What's wrong with me?"

"You have baby wings back here," he said as he shifted.

She felt his finger trace along something that felt like a curve on her back and she blushed with pleasure.

"I have wings?" she squeaked.

"They're tiny little harpy wings. I don't think you'll be able to fly with them, but they're there."

"I don't want wings, Tyler. I want to be normal."

He leaned down and brushed his lips along her back and wings, forcing her belly to quiver.

"Tyler..."

"Did you like that?" he asked.

"What are you doing to me?"

"Just touching you. But it's good to know that these are so sensitive. Now, try to imagine your wings are gone and maybe they'll go back into your back so you can hide them."

She did as she was told, even though thoughts of his touch and the fact that she was completely and utterly changing in more ways than one plagued her mind. Abby's body shuddered again and she felt something sharp slide into her back though it didn't hurt.

"There, you did it, baby." He shifted again and slid her shirt back down.

She still couldn't believe this was happening, but in case it was still a dream, she didn't want to move too much and accidently wake up. Tyler Cooper was holding her close and now she looked like a harpy, even though she could hide the affects somewhat.

She could ignore the latter for now—she had to if she wanted to stay sane.

Tyler shuffled something on the table by them and picked up some candy hearts. He blushed and handed her one. "Sorry, I'm addicted to the things."

"Must come from being a cupid, right? Oh, and I love them, too." She popped one in her mouth and gagged. A rotten taste settled on her tongue and she spit the candy out. "Oh, God, sorry about that. It just tasted...like trash or something."

Tyler moved to look at her, worry in his gaze. He popped one in his mouth and shook his head. "It tastes fine to me, but I think I know what the issue is."

Abby frowned. "Is it some harpy thing? Oh, God, what's wrong with me?" An irrational anger spread through her, scaring her. She wasn't an angry person. Well she hadn't been before... She took a deep breath, suppressing the urge to scream or hit something. Again, not like her at all.

Oh, God, she was changing

"I think it has to do with being a harpy, yes. From what I've read in the past, harpies can only eat food they've stolen, so you won't be able to eat anything I give you or you make yourself."

"No, that can't be right. How can I live like that?"

"We'll find a way. I mean, if I leave something out and tell you it's mine and mine alone, I think you can eat it; or if you eat from my plate. It'll come to us."

"I don't think I can do this."

"You're stronger than you think you are, Abigail."

"I'm going to be, aren't I?" Abby frowned and looked at the man she loved, even if she didn't know if she could in the future. "How do you know so much about harpies anyway?"

Tyler blushed. Yes, the hunky, strong, alpha sheriff blushed and ducked his head. "I read a lot about the supernatural and other things. It's like a hobby...or a fascination. Even though I don't really know much about being a cupid and Aeneas. I guess I just ignored that part. You know, ignoring my future and all that."

Abby smiled and touched his chin. "I like that you like the things no one believes."

"We live in Holiday; I can't *not* believe it. Plus, even as a boy, I wanted to read about the histories of werewolves and dragons."

"You think those exist?"

Tyler shook his head. "I have no idea, but I think it would be cool. What I do know is that we're going to figure out how to be a cupid and a harpy together. Okay?"

"This is all so weird. I mean, you were ignoring me like yesterday, and now look at us."

Tyler frowned. "I know. I don't like magic right now. It's made us lose so much time."

"I can't believe everything that's happened. I was just at home packing..." Her words trailed off, and her eyes widened. "I'm moving."

Tyler's eyes grew stormy. "No, you're not."

"Excuse me? You can't tell me what to

do."

"No, I can't, but how could you move now?"

"I wasn't moving because of you, Tyler." Okay, that was a lie. She had been moving because of him, at least partially, but now everything had changed, not only because someone might want her but because she had changed.

She wasn't human anymore.

How could she live anywhere else when everything was in such a state of flux?

"I know you weren't. You said it was because you had nothing here. But you do, Abigail. Don't you see that? Even if we leave me out of the equation, which I don't want you to do, you have a family here. We Coopers don't want to let you go."

"Why couldn't you have said that before I put my house up for sale?"

"Because I couldn't. I didn't know."

"I can't move, can I?"

"I don't want you to. And I don't know what's going on with the effects of the arrow, baby. I think you should stay."

She let out a breath, fear and anxiety filling her. "I haven't sold my place yet, and I don't have a lease in Denver. I don't *have* to move. Plus, Justin hasn't replaced me at work yet..."

"That's what Brayden said about your place."

"You're talking about me with your brothers?"

Tyler kissed her brow, and tingles shot up her spine. "Yep. Brayden already knows what's going on. And since we Coopers gossip like old hens, I'm pretty sure the rest of my brothers and Jordan knows."

"Do they know what happened to me?" she asked as her tension escalated. What would they think of her? What if what Aeneas said was true and she lost what made her nice and kind?

"Not yet, but we'll tell them together. You're not alone anymore, Abigail."

Oh, how she wanted to believe in that, but she couldn't. Not yet, anyway.

Tyler brushed her lips with his own, bringing a sense of peace to her. "I'll prove it to you, baby."

But, what if he couldn't?

Chapter 9

"Just keep your eye on the ball," Tyler said as he wrapped his arms around Abigail, liking the way her bottom pressed against his groin. Her wings were tucked into her back so he could pull her closer and not worry about crushing the fragile, surprisingly sensitive things.

"I bet you say that to all the girls." She laughed and wiggled in his hold.

His cock sprang to attention, the zipper on his jeans sure to leave a mark. Holy hell, this woman made him hot.

He couldn't wait to strip her down, bend her over something, and sink into her heat.

Soon.

Tyler nipped at her ear, and she jumped, almost hitting him on the head with the bat.

"Okay, maybe I should show you how to hit before you give me a concussion," he teased then kissed her cheek. He lingered, inhaling her scent of roses.

Damn, he wanted her for more than just a night.

For some reason, that didn't scare him at all.

It had been a week since everything had happened. Though Abigail had gone back to her place after a sweaty encounter on his couch, they were still practically joined at the hip. He didn't want to miss any more time.

She seemed to take it in stride, but he

could feel her cautiousness. He knew she didn't quite believe his sudden change, but that was okay. It was a dramatic one, and he needed to prove to her that he loved her.

That he always had.

That is was just magic that had messed everything up.

Yes, it seemed almost impossible, but he'd fix it. He loved this woman and tried to show her in everything he did. They ate almost every meal together, either at his place, her home, or at the diner.

Though the times they ate at the diner, he could sense her fear. Considering she had to eat off his plate in secret, it made it a little odd. Her claws only came out when she felt frightened or angry and her wings only came out when they needed to breathe after a long day tucked in her back—much like his own wings.

For some reason, the town seemed enamored by the playboy and the "nothing romance."

Yes, that's what the town newspaper called it.

He'd paid a visit to the editor the next morning and had some words. Luckily, Brayden had been there to hold him back so he hadn't used his fists instead, though it was close.

The town didn't quite know what to do with the fact that Tyler and Abigail were dating and seemed to be farther in their relationship than would normally occur in just a week. Some thought it was a pity thing on Tyler's part because she was moving, even though Abigail had told everyone she was staying.

That had led to people whispering that she'd stayed for him and was desperate enough to stay for a man.

Neither of them had set the record straight and told the gossipers that she'd stayed because she was now a harpy, not only because of him.

He'd like to think she'd stayed for him just a little. He'd told her he'd move to Denver if she wanted, and she'd freaked. She'd told him that she'd been crazy and her claws and wings had popped out. Apparently, he'd moved a little too fast for her and she hadn't been able to control her emotions. Thankfully, they'd been at her place and not in public. From now on he'd have to make sure he didn't upset her in public.

Okay, so it had been a little too soon to mention that since the Coopers always lived in Holiday, he was the freaking sheriff, and he also had cupid responsibilities. But, he'd have moved for her.

He'd backed off when she'd tried to run away from him and back off their relationship.

No sense in scaring her more than he already had.

The other women in town were viscous in their attitudes toward Abigail, and although Tyler would never hit a woman, he'd been tempted a few times with some of those shrews. They'd gone as far as to say that Tyler only stayed because Abigail would spread her legs for him in a certain way that made her a novelty compared to his past.

Fucking bitches.

He and Abigail hadn't even made it that far in their relationship. He knew she was a virgin and wanted to take it slow.

Though his cock ached and he'd had perpetual blue balls for the past week, he'd take it. Abigail was important to him. She must have always been, but Aeneas's spell had hidden that fact from him.

Anger coursed through his veins thinking about the fucking anti-Cupid, or whatever the hell he was. That man had taken so much from them, and Tyler couldn't find him. He, Justin, and Brayden had gone back to the cabin the next day and looked for the bastard, but he was long gone.

He'd done his research on Aeneas, at least the man he knew as Aeneas and had come up with nothing. His search had only come up with a few men and a minor god, not anything that really could be what they were dealing with. Tyler kept those on the backburner just in case. He'd followed the trail as far as he could, but it turned cold. At this point, he was out of options unless he turned to the other cupids. He had no idea how to contact other cupids or Frank, but he was looking for a way to do so.

Maybe they'd be able to at least give him information on Aeneas.

Tyler had a feeling it was far from over since the lunatic wanted Tyler in pain, but at least they had a reprieve. Tyler didn't want to leave Abigail alone for too long though, even though he knew he was just using that as an excuse to stay longer with her.

No matter. He wanted this woman in his life, in his heart, and in his bed.

He just hoped Abigail felt the same. Even though she'd said the words, he couldn't be sure until he knew she knew he was serious and that the whole harpy change wouldn't be an issue.

They were not at the batting cages for another date. He loved sports. If something could be hit, dunked, thrown, or tackled, he was in. Abigail, on the other hand, hated them and would rather swim or dance.

The fact that she'd do this for him? He loved it.

"You okay, Tyler?" Abigail asked as she lowered the bat and turned in his arms.

He looked down into her hazel eyes and fell just that much more in love. God, he sounded like a cheesy, lovesick poet, but whatever. This was his Abigail.

Tyler traced his finger along her cheek, loving the way she shuddered. "Yeah, I'm fine. Just thinking about the past week."

Anger, confusion, happiness, and sadness warred in her eyes. "It's been an interesting week, for sure."

"Interesting? That's the best word you can use?" he growled as he lifted her by her hips to kiss her.

God, her taste... He could drown in it.

"Slut," a woman whispered behind them, and Tyler slowly let Abigail down to the ground, even as he noticed the stiffness in her body.

Tyler turned toward the woman. Natalie, he thought her name was. Yes, he was sure of it. He'd turned her down a while back because he didn't like to date in town anymore, too messy.

Well, he supposed it got messy no matter what happened.

"Excuse me?" he asked, his voice low, controlled.

Natalie's eyes widened a fraction then narrowed into slits. "Just saying what the town's thinking. Of all women, Abigail? Scraping the bottom of the barrel, aren't you?"

Damn it to hell. He knew the town thought that Abigail wasn't good enough for him since he was a fucking Cooper, but they couldn't be farther from the truth. He was the one not good enough for her. He was pretty sure the town was acting like this because they wanted him to be with one of the town's darlings like Natalie.

Damn them for matchmaking and getting it beyond wrong.

He felt Abigail behind him, though she didn't move, didn't speak. Fuck, he hated when anything caused her pain. He felt her hand on his back, tension radiating from her body. He knew it was his fault that Natalie was spewing lies and crap, hurting his Abigail. He'd just have to be the one to fix it. Nothing hurt her and walked away.

"You need to go now, Natalie."

"Whatever. When you're done with that piece of trash, because you will be—that girl could never hold your attention—come call me. I'm not some fat piece of ass who couldn't get a date before and must have something on you."

The park had gone quiet, and he felt Abigail clutch his shirt.

"Okay, you are so off the mark it's not even funny, Natalie. Just because you're jealous of something you never had a chance in hell in having doesn't mean you can act like the bitch you are. Now fucking apologize to Abigail."

"Make me."

"Oh, that's mature," Abigail said as she went up to the fence. "Get away. Nobody needs you here. I'm sorry you're so insecure you feel the need to lash out at anyone with a pulse, but get over yourself. I know I'm not skinny like you, but I'm pretty sure Tyler likes my curves."

"Hell, yeah," he agreed, liking the way his Abigail stood up for herself.

"He's just saying that because he wants you on your back again," Natalie spat.

"Oh, shut up. Can you see that you're not wanted here? Nothing you can say can hurt me, Natalie. I've heard it all before." She raised her voice and looked out onto the crowd. "I know I'm not the typical girl for a Cooper man, but hell, you guys never saw me to begin with. So, just go about your business because I'm tired of having to hide because you are all insecure about your own lives."

She turned to Tyler and smiled, though

he could see the tension in her shoulders. "Want to go home? I'm not in the mood to hit anything anymore. Well, at least not a ball." She glared at Natalie, and Tyler was pretty sure he saw something different flare in her eyes. A blue flame sputtered around the iris, sending shockwaves through his system.

Fuck, he'd forgotten for a moment she was a harpy now, and they still didn't know the extent of her powers.

Tyler leaned down and kissed her. "Sure thing, baby. Let's go to my place. We can eat there." He tangled his fingers with hers and walked toward his SUV, leaving the townsfolk and Natalie staring back open-mouthed.

As they got in the SUV and started toward his place, he kissed her palm. "That was sexy as hell, Abigail."

"Really? Well, I'm shaking. I hate confrontation. I can't believe I said all that."

"I'm glad you did. She had no right to say anything about you."

Abigail let out a breath. "Well, we did kind of spring this on them."

Tyler pulled into his parking spot and

got out of the car, immediately going to Abigail's side so he could kiss her.

"Shut up," he said playfully. "Don't make excuses for them. So what if we did? We're not hurting anyone, and we're dating. It's not like we're attacking anyone or walking around naked." He raised a brow. "Though the latter sounds fun."

Abigail threw her head back and laughed. "Is that all you think about?"

Tyler smiled and kissed her thoroughly on his porch. "Pretty much. Well, that and sports. Oh, and food."

"Typical guy."

"You know you love me," he teased.

"Yeah, I guess I do," she whispered.

Tyler froze then leaned down closer, his heart beating so fast he was sure it would explode out his chest like in those old cartoons.

"Really?"

"Yeah, don't get a big head about it or anything. You already knew, anyway."

"Yeah, but I didn't know if you still did

since everything changed."

"I love you, Tyler Cooper."

"I love you, too, Abigail Clarke."

He leaned down and kissed her, their mouths meshing, and his heart falling for her again.

"God, get a room," Clara, his married neighbor, lashed out behind him.

Tyler groaned and turned toward the bitter woman. Jesus, what was it with the women in this town?

"What do you want, Clara?" Tyler asked, not really caring.

"Do you have to flaunt your... whatever the hell you want to call it with that nobody... wherever people can see it?"

Tyler let out a breath, tired of all this shit. He could have sworn people loved Abigail before he started dating her, but now people were acting like jealous bitches. "You know what, Clara? Go home to your husband and stop trying to rub your body on me. Stop talking shit about Abigail and, for once in your life, leave me the fuck alone."

Clara gasped. "You've never yelled at me before. It must because of *her*."

"Oh, shut up," Abigail growled. "Tyler already told me about the way you flaunt yourself and throw yourself at him even though you're married. If you're really that unhappy in your marriage, I'm sorry. But, I'm more sorry for your husband for the way you don't respect him or yourself or your marriage. Stop trying to get in the way of things that aren't your concern and just back the fuck away."

Abigail yelled the last part, her hands curling into talons, claws coming out of her fingertips, and Tyler pulled her back ever so slightly, trying to hide the change. He looked down at her back and held back a wince. Her wings were out in full force, fluttering away in her anger.

Apparently, the anger and standing up for their relationship and herself had caused the harpy within her to come out.

"Are you going to let her talk to me that way?" Clara asked as she backed away.

Seriously? Why did these women think he had any influence on what Abigail said? She was her own woman and independent, even if the town couldn't see that. Even if *he* hadn't been able to see that.

"Go home, Clara," he said as he purposefully turned his side to her and led Abigail into the apartment. He wouldn't give the bitch his back. He didn't trust her not to come at him, guns blazing.

"I can't believe these women, Tyler. Is it always going to be like this?"

"I never dated either of them, actually."

Abigail threw her hands up. "Oh, yeah, because that makes it so much better. What's going to happen when we actually see someone you slept with? And don't call it dating. We both know you never did that."

Shame filled him. He'd never regretted his past, not until he'd found Abigail.

"Abigail..."

"No, don't worry. I know you have a past; I knew it going in. I'm not jealous." She gave a harsh laugh. "Okay, maybe just a little. But I'm a big enough person to get over it and not let it affect us. Okay?"

He went to her, pulled her into his arms,

and inhaled her fresh rose scent. "I'm sorry she ruined our declarations."

Abigail snorted. "Nah, she didn't do too much."

"I hate to bring this up, but did you see your hands when you yelled at her?" As much as he wanted to hold her and ignore the rest, they had to get a handle on her new powers—or whatever they wanted to call them.

He felt her nod, even as her body shuddered. He walked her toward the kitchen, needing to get her away from the door. "Yes, I felt them, too. They're gone now. I guess I'm going to have to learn to control this new temper of mine."

Her voice broke at the end, and he lifted her up in his arms so he could set her on the kitchen counter. Tyler stood between her legs and cupped her face.

"You're learning to make them go away, that's better than nothing. You're already doing well in hiding it, too. And as for your temper, I love everything about you. You stood up for yourself, for us. You're perfect."

"Shut up. I'm not perfect, but I'll take the standing-up-for-us part. I don't like the way those women acted. I just hope I don't act like that when—" Her eyes widened as she cut herself off.

"When what?" he asked, afraid to hear the answer.

She swallowed hard. "When you figure out it was all a mistake and you leave me," she whispered.

His heart broke even as anger coursed through him. He gripped her chin and tilted her head up so he could look into those hazel eyes he loved so much.

"I'm not leaving you, Abigail. Not now, not ever. I'm a cupid; I know love when I see it. I'm not walking away, no matter what happens. Do you understand me? And I'm getting a little tired of feeling like I've done something to cause you to doubt me."

"Do I need to point out the last few years?" she said sharply then shook her head, looking as if she held back her temper. Damn, before her change, she hadn't had this issue he didn't think, but he still loved her. In fact, she looked damn hot when she was angry.

"It's only been a week, Tyler. And I know you feel something. I feel it, too. But what if it all goes away?"

"Life can change in an instant. We both know that." An image of his parents' accident came to mind, but he brushed it away. Not the time. "I'm not leaving, Abigail. I love you."

She leaned back and smiled. "I love you too." She let out a breath. "Okay, I need to get over myself and just let things happen because worrying is only hurting us both."

"I'll try not to let my insecurities do the same."

"What?"

"I'm afraid you'll figure out you can do better than a man who can't advance in his job, who spent too many years doing things he now regrets, and is ten years older than you."

"Okay, well, that's just stupid. I loved you when you did all that in the past, so I don't know what the problem is. You love your job, and you're amazing at it. We're both going to get over our pasts, and as for the age thing, it's not like I'm a kid. I know how old you are, and it doesn't bother me."

"I'm practically an old man."

Abigail rolled her eyes and wrapped her legs around his waist. "Oh, yes, I can just see the social security checks coming. You're thirty-two, Tyler. I'm twenty-two. But in terms of who we are, we're the same age. I mean, we haven't spent a lot of time in committed relationships, so we can take it one step at a time. That's all that matters."

He leaned down and brushed his lips across her. "I'm still too old for you."

"Get over it." She sank into his hold, and he kissed her again.

God, he loved her taste.

She tightened her hold, and he ran his hands up and down her back, sliding up under her shirt and feeling the softness of her skin. She pulled him closer, and he rocked his erection against the seam of her jeans, sending shivers along both of them.

They'd made out a few times, kissed constantly, but hadn't taken it any further. He needed to stop now because in another few minutes he wouldn't be able to, not when he had the epitome of perfection in his arms.

Tyler pulled back, his breath coming in heavy pants. "We need to stop."

She looked up at him, her eyes wide, her pupils dilated with need. "I don't want to."

His knees shook. "Are you sure?"

"I'm ready; I've *been* ready. Please, Tyler. I want you so much."

His cock stood up at attention and throbbed. Jesus, he had to calm down. The last thing he needed was to come in his jeans like a teenager before he even had a chance to show Abigail what making love was.

And it would be making love.

And fucking.

Because no matter what, he'd make sure it was fucking hot.

Tyler was afraid to speak but picked her up and carried her to the bedroom.

"Damn, shouldn't I have candles or flowers or something?" He set her on her feet, his body a coil ready to spring. "This is your first time. It needs to be special, baby."

Abby smiled and kissed under his chin. "I'm so happy that I'm not the only nervous one right now. But Tyler, shut up and make love to me, okay? I know anything we do will be special. Just kiss me."

"God, I love you," he said as he crashed his mouth to hers, wanting to taste her, wanting his skin to smell like her and hers to smell like his.

God, talk about animalistic.

He ran his hands up and down her body, feeling her curves, loving the fact that she wasn't a twig and had something he could grab onto. He pulled back and kissed along her chin and down her neck. Her breaths came in little pants as she gripped his arms, needy.

"I want to taste you," he growled, and she shuddered.

He knelt before her and slowly stripped off her top, leaving her in her lacy white bra, her breasts full and ready, the nipples poking out between the flowers on the cups.

Holy fuck.

"Jesus, baby, you're beautiful."

She blushed all over and ran a hand through his hair. "I know I have curves, I hope that's okay.

"It's better than okay," he grunted.

"Then be gentle. Or not."

"Damn, baby." He cupped her breasts and kneaded them, loving the little moans she made as he rolled her nipples. "I'm going to taste these, real soon."

He undid her jeans and slid them down her legs as she shucked off the little flats she wore. Her panties matched her bra, and Tyler was pretty sure there was drool on his chin.

"Fuck."

"Is that all you can say?" she asked as she swayed from foot to foot, clearly nervous.

He placed his hands on her hips and looked up at her. "You're amazing. And you're mine."

"Yours."

He nodded at her acceptance and kissed her panties, inhaling. Oh, fuck, yeah, he was gonna taste her tonight. Soon.

"Tyler," she whispered, and he knew she was getting wetter, or at least he hoped so.

"It's just the beginning." He got to his feet and kissed her, hard.

She wrapped her arms around him, and her breasts brushed against his shirt, her heated core flame hot along his jeans.

He walked her back to the bed and sat her on the edge. She gasped as he let his thumb brush against her neck, her pulse fast, needy. Without speaking, he undid her bra, letting her breasts fall, heavy, needing his tongue. He loved the size, the shape...the feel. She was natural, a beauty. His.

Tyler knelt and cupped her breasts, the rosy peaks begging for his tongue. With a heated breath, he let the flat of his tongue press against her right nipple, then her left. The bud tightened against him and he flicked them softly. As he licked each one, Abigail shuddered, her body breaking out in goose bumps. He sucked harder; wanting to make sure she felt it deep down in her pussy, knowing with the size of them, he'd have to make sure she could feel everything because of lack of sensitivity.

But, damn, was she responsive.

She moaned, her legs moving against him as he pressed her breasts closer. Oh, his Abigail wanted more.

That he could arrange.

He sucked harder, nibbling just a little as she squirmed. He pulled back as she looked up at him, just on the brink.

"Have you come before?"

She nodded and blushed. "Yes, I mean, I have toys, just not any that penetrate."

Fuck. "You're full of surprises. You about to come in my arms just then? That was fucking hot. Next time we go to your place and we use them, okay?"

Her eyes darkened. "Deal, but please make me come. I don't think I can just from my breasts."

"I know, baby, it's okay. I'm going to taste you, lick every part of you, and you'll come. Then I'm going to sink into you. I know it's going to hurt, baby, but I'm going to do my best to make sure all you feel is me and goodness, okay?"

He kissed down her belly, lingering above her panties, then slowly rolled them down her legs.

Oh, shit, he needed to think about

something to hold him back. Baseball, Grandma, a cat...anything. He didn't want to come right there.

But, his Abigail was beautiful. Her light brown curls framed a pink pussy that begged for his lips, then his cock.

He traced her outer lips, loving the way she moaned. "Oh, God, Abigail, I don't know how I'm going to wait."

"Then don't."

He smiled. "Deal." Tyler pushed her back softly and lay between her legs and gave her pussy one long swipe. She thrashed, and he chuckled. "You taste fantastic. Like something sweet, something mine."

Tyler went back to his meal, licking, sucking, and nibbling, then inserted a finger, then another. Hell, she was tight, but wet, and his.

He increased his pace as he felt her walls clamp down on him, and she screamed his name. He kept his mouth on her, wanting to taste every drop but looked up when she rolled her own nipples between her fingers as she came.

Now that was fucking hot.

He pulled back and stripped down, watching the way she gazed as his chest, his legs, and his cock. He knew he had a decent body, had to with his job, but the way she looked at him?

Yeah, he felt like a god.

Now to prove it.

He quickly went to his nightstand, put on a condom, and took a deep breath. He was afraid he'd come as soon as she surrounded him. Not to mention the fact that he was scared to hurt her. He'd already done it enough.

Worry crossed her features, and she held out a hand. "Tyler, it's all right. You can't hurt me."

Tyler slowly pushed her up so she was lying in the middle of the bed, her hair framed around her like a goddess. He moved so he was kneeling between her legs again, hovering over her. "It's going to hurt."

"Then you can make it better," she teased.

He leaned down and captured her lips.

She moaned in surprise, and he chuckled.

"Like the way you taste?"

"I like the way I taste on you. I can't wait to return the favor."

He groaned and almost came. "Fuck, baby, we'll save that for next time, okay? I can't wait to see your lips wrapped around my dick, but let's take care of you first."

"I love it when you talk dirty."

"Good because I don't plan to stop."

Tyler moved so his cock slightly brushed her, and she gasped. Oh, hell, yeah, this was gonna be good. He moved slowly, oh so slowly, groaning as she tightened on him. When he reached her barrier, he kissed her and thrust, hard.

She gasped in pain, and he stilled, waiting for her body to accommodate him.

"Abigail?"

"I'm fine. I'm more than fine. We're connected, Tyler."

He smiled, his body warming with more than just need. "Yes, baby, we are. I'm going to move, okay? You ready?"

"Oh, God yes, fuck me, Tyler."

He laughed and moved back, watching the awe on her face as he did so. "I love it when you talk dirty to me."

"Good because I don't plan to stop," she said.

He thrust in and out, slowly at first, then harder when he couldn't help himself. He watched as her body blushed, peaking over her own crest as his back tingled, sending a shot to his balls, and his dick throbbed, and he came.

He felt the tingle in his back from where his wings threatened to come out right along with his orgasm. Apparently, all of his magic was connected, but he'd deal with that later.

Tyler didn't stop moving, wanting to make sure she maintained her wave of pleasure until they both lay in a pile, his softening cock still embedded in her heat.

"I love you," she whispered and snuggled closer.

"I love you," he said and ran a hand down her sweat-slicked back.

God, that was different. Perfect. Theirs.

He couldn't wait to do it again.

Chapter 10

"Why am I so nervous about dinner?" Abby asked the next day. She smoothed her dress, the hem reaching to mid-thigh, just below the stockings she planned to share with Tyler later that night.

She blushed at the thought of his hands, lips, and tongue on places that she'd saved just for him. Who knew sex could be so much fun?

Okay, fine, everyone knew that, but she wasn't a virgin anymore. She was surprised the town hadn't thrown a parade or something for her. Knowing them, it'd have a banner proudly letting the world know that Tyler had made a woman out of her in big bold script. And, of course, the other ladies in town would have signs calling her the names they'd already said to her face.

Abby blocked those images, letting the one of Tyler fill her thoughts. Yes, he was better to think about anyway. Though everything had moved so fast that she was afraid to even blink, she was happy.

Thoughts of what would happen once things spiraled downward tried to claw at her, but she ignored them. She'd promised Tyler that she'd live in the moment and only think of a future filled with happiness—with him. She'd do it too. There was no use thinking that everything could fall apart at any moment because she needed to let everything sink in.

"You shouldn't be nervous about dinner, Abigail," Tyler said as he leaned down to kiss her neck.

Shivers skated over her, and she closed her eyes on a moan. Apparently, she *really* liked sex, as in wanting it all the freaking time. Even his touch would turn her on in an instant. She could have blamed her addiction on the fact that she was now a harpy, and, apparently, they were sexual beings, but she had a feeling that it was just her.

She had a lot of ground to make up for, and Tyler seemed to want to make sure she covered it. They'd made love twice more in the night, and though she was sore, she still wanted more. And by the feel of his touch and the front of his jeans, he was just as needy.

"I'm nervous because this is a Cooper family dinner, Tyler. It's not just going out and casually meeting up with them. No, this is the dinner that's for *family* only."

"So? You should have been coming for a while now. You're practically family as it is."

Abby scrunched her face and let out a sigh-like growl. "That isn't helping, you know. I know your brothers already know what's going on with us and our...paranormal activities, but it's not the same as a dinner. They're going to look at us differently. And what if they don't treat me the same?"

Tyler looked adorably confused and brushed a piece of hair behind her ear. "What are you talking about? My brothers would never hurt you. They might act odd or unsure, but I don't think hurting would ever be a part of it."

"But, they always treated me like a sister, even though I never went to any of their dinners. I'm just their friend really. Now that I'm with you, what if they treat me differently? Like harsher because they're looking out for you or something?"

Tyler threw his head back and laughed, and she punched him in the shoulder.

"What the hell? Why are you laughing at me? There's a real reason I'm freaking out, and you're *laughing*? Maybe I should go because *you're* the one acting like an ass." She folded her arms over her chest and glared at the man she'd planned on jumping later that night. Well, not anymore.

Tyler shook his head and tried to lean down to kiss her, but she moved out of his reach.

"Oh, no you don't, Tyler Cooper. Tell me why you thought it was appropriate to laugh when I have real worries."

"Baby, think about it. You're the one they're going to defend, not me."

"Huh?"

"They love you like one of our own. Just not the way I love you." Yes, that little warmth spread through her at those words, but that wasn't the point. "They're going to protect you from me and make sure that you're taken care of. I'm surprised they haven't beaten me already for how I treated you."

"Seriously? You need to stop beating yourself over that. We're looking forward, remember?"

Tyler leaned down to kiss her, and she let him. "I know. I just wanted to remind you that the Coopers take care of their own. And you're one of us."

That happy warmth slid to all the places in her heart and soul that had long since frozen when her parents ignored her. She was a Cooper by association, but not fully family. Maybe one day...if Tyler...

No, she didn't want to worry about that. Not when they'd been together only a handful of days. Though she'd loved him for so long, it was like a dream.

"I like the sound of that," she finally said and leaned against Tyler's dresser. She'd brought her knit dress and other daily necessities to get ready at his house, though Tyler had said he wanted to spend more time at hers.

It made sense since she owned a house while he only had a small apartment. She'd even bought the darn thing so she could raise a family and build a larger home. Maybe he'd help create a home with her.

Okay, she really needed to stop daydreaming about homes and children based on only his teasing smile. Her ovaries weren't going to be able to take much more.

"Good, you better like the sound of that" Tyler said as he walked her to the front entryway so they could put on their coats.

"Do we need to bring anything other than this?" she asked as she nodded toward the bottle of wine and case of beer.

Tyler shook his head. "No, usually we don't even bring the wine, but now that you, Rina, and Jordan are there, we decided to venture out."

"Classy," she said dryly. "So, Justin's doing all the cooking?" she asked as they piled into the SUV, complete with the drinks and a large duffel bag of Tyler's clothes.

That giddy feeling of things going right wrapped around her again.

Tyler drove toward the Cooper place, once their parents' house but now Jackson's home. The property was set off from Holiday a good ten miles or so but had to be one of the most beautiful places ever. Once Jackson settled down, he'd have a great home to raise his family. She knew the rest of the brothers had always planned on building homes of their own so they could grow and continue the Cooper clan.

Matt used to live in a small apartment above his hardware store but now lived in one of the old, large houses in town that belonged to his wife, Jordan. Though, if you asked Jordan now, she'd have said the house belonged to both of them. When Jordan's aunt had died, she'd come back to town to clean it out and had never left.

Thank God.

Justin lived in a small house close to the school and was planning on building on with Matt's help. His fiancée, Rina, had a home at the North Pole, which she'd keep so they could visit up there.

Abigail couldn't wait to join them and see where Santa lived. She couldn't help it. She was a dreamer like that. She wouldn't have been with Tyler if she weren't.

Brayden lived on the other side of town, which in Holiday meant that he lived about twenty minutes away; in a large house he and Matt had designed and built themselves. Abby had no idea why the place was so large, but she knew it needed a family, particularly Allison and her kids, but she wouldn't tell Brayden that.

They pulled up to Jackson's, and Abby smiled. She could do this. It was just a family dinner even though it was the first one she'd been invited to.

She would not squeal and do a cheer. No, she'd leave that to the inner cheerleader who was currently shaking her booty like she had nothing else to do.

Oh, if Tyler only knew the thoughts in

her head, he'd leave her in a second. Probably on the front steps of the psych ward.

"Ready for this?" Tyler asked as he opened her door.

Wow, she must have really been in her head because she hadn't even noticed him getting out of the SUV.

"Yep. But don't leave my side, okay?" She winced at the sound of desperation in her voice and bit her lip.

Tyler leaned in and kissed her, his lips firm, yet gentle. "Never."

Okay, then.

They walked through the door without knocking, something that made Abby smile. She loved that about this family, the way they were just there for each other and didn't care about locked doors and unwanted guests. At least with each other. The rest of the town was another matter.

"Abby!" Jordan yelled across the room as she ran toward her. "You're here!" The other woman brought Abby into a huge hug, and Abby almost dropped the wine she was holding.

"Watch the wine, dear," Matt said as he laughed and took the bottle from Abby's hands before laying a kiss on her cheek.

"Oh, God! I almost broke the wine. What would we have done?" Jordan said as she rolled her eyes. "It isn't as if Jackson doesn't have his own wine cabinet or anything." Jordan winked, and Matt kissed her fully.

Oh, the lovebirds.

Tyler came up behind her and wrapped his arm around her waist. "Making trouble already, are we?" he asked, his breath tickling her ear in the sexiest way possible.

Okay, so this dinner might take a little too long for comfort.

They greeted the rest of the brothers and Rina then sat down at the dinner table, drinks and appetizers in hand.

Only she couldn't really eat anything on the table. Not really.

Damn harpy genetics.

They'd found a way around it though, thankfully, but only the Coopers and Allison knew what it was. Meaning things were interesting in public.

All the others had to do was mention that their plate belonged to them or make it clear to Abby that she couldn't have any. Then she could take from their plate.

She didn't feel comfortable doing it to anyone else, so she really only ate off of Tyler's plate. But, still, it was awkward as hell.

She'd just have to get over it.

Abby "snuck" a piece of brie off of Tyler's plate and moaned around it. God, Justin was a fabulous cook. Good for Rina.

Tyler pretended not to notice and ate some of the brie on his own. She could do this. It was just *really* different from anything else she'd known. But it was Holiday. Most things *were* different.

"What are your plans for the wedding?" Matt asked as he wrapped his arm around Jordan's chair.

Both Abby and Tyler choked on their crackers, bringing laughter to the people at the table.

"I was asking Justin and Rina," Matt

clarified. "But, good to know that you're thinking about marriage." He winked, and Tyler growled at him then threw a roll.

"Stop fucking throwing things at the dinner table," Jackson reprimanded.

"Stop fucking cussing at the dinner table," Brayden teased, and they broke into laughter.

Yep, she loved the Coopers.

"Okay, then, back to the wedding," Justin said as he took a sip of his beer. "We're planning on having a small one."

He took a bite of cheese, and the rest of the family looked at him.

"And?" Jordan asked, laughter in her eyes.

"What?"

Rina rolled her eyes and kissed under his chin. She'd forgone the glamor that she usually wore so everyone could see her pointed ears that, for some reason, Justin loved to play with.

"We're going to invite just family, but of course that includes Abby, Allison, and her kids." She smiled, and Abby warmed. "We want it to be in the backyard here. Is that okay, Jackson?"

They all turned to the head of the table where Jackson played with the bottle of beer in his hand, not really paying attention.

Or so she thought.

"I'm fine with that. This is Cooper land. I think the folks would have liked that," he said, his voice low and that one statement holding more emotion than she'd heard in anything else he'd ever said in her presence.

The rest of the room grew quiet as they thought of the Coopers who'd passed away. It seemed like only a moment ago, but had been years.

Justin cleared his throat then kissed the tear running down Rina's cheek while Tyler did the same to Abby. Even though she knew Rina hadn't known the Coopers, anything that hurt Justin touched Rina.

"Thank you," Justin finally said. "You won't have to worry about a party here. We're planning on heading right up to the North Pole for the reception. I think the kids will like it." Abby knew Justin was speaking of Allison's children.

"Oh, I love that idea," Abby said.

"Yes, I so can't wait to see the North Pole," Jordan added.

"Great, it's settled then. Since Tyler has to be here for Valentine's Day, we were planning to go up after that. We thought we'd have the wedding on the twentieth. Does that sound okay?"

"So soon?" Jordan asked and Abby agreed it seemed too fast to plan a wedding.

Rina smiled. "We don't need much. We just want to be husband and wife. Plus, this way, we can enjoy the rest of the year together before we have to buckle down again in November."

"Makes sense," Tyler said.

Jordan and Rina smiled at him, and Abby growled.

How dare they look at her man?

The people around her quieted and widened their eyes.

Oh, God, where had that thought come

from?

Tyler took her hand and kissed her palm. "It's okay, Abby. They're family."

She nodded, tears springing to her eyes. Aeneas had been right. This was what he'd taken from her.

Her kindness.

And, apparently, her sanity.

"It's just the harpy thing, right?" Jordan asked. "You don't want us encroaching on your territory?"

Abby let out a shaky breath. "Apparently. Sorry, really. I'm trying to tone it down. I've already yelled at some of the horde of women following him around."

The Coopers broke out into laughter.

"Oh, God, I love you, Abby, darling," Brayden said, wiping a tear from his eye.

"Watch your mouth, brother mine," Tyler growled.

Brayden just rolled his eyes. "I'm not poaching. Get over yourself. And really, a horde? I love it. Now, let's eat. I want to make sure Abby doesn't eat from my plate."

He winked at her, and she smiled.

Looked like she had two plates to eat from.

As they ate, they talked of the upcoming wedding and Tyler's new job as cupid. She loved the fact that they could all be open with each other about the things that didn't seem normal.

Well, at least all except Brayden and Jackson. They both looked like they were hiding things, but this wasn't the time to bother them about it.

"So, no pink tutu?" Brayden asked as he looked away from his plate so Abby could steal a bite of chicken.

"Fuck you," Tyler said as he looked away from his roll.

Seriously, these two were going to fatten her up if they didn't start trying to eat food off their own plates.

"So, you just feel the love and *boom*... hit them with an arrow?" Justin asked.

"You say that sarcastically, but aren't

you the one who can feel the holiday cheer?" Tyler drawled.

"Point for you."

"It's just a feeling I have, and I don't have it with everyone. But the two weeks before Valentine's Day are, apparently, the busiest days of the year for me, though I'll always have to deal with the fact that I may have to shoot someone with an arrow. I keep them in my SUV just in case."

Things were sure different in Holiday.

By the time they finished eating and hanging out, it was almost ten when they left and got to her place. Though she was tired and full, she still wanted to show Tyler her stockings.

Wanton much?

She walked into her living room, watching as Tyler set down his bag, looking right at home in her place, or at least, she'd felt like he belonged there by her side. For some reason, that didn't scare her in the slightest.

No, it felt right.

Perfect.

Let's just hope things don't change.

Abby frowned as Tyler scratched his back for what had to be the hundredth time that night. At first she'd ignored it, but now, she realized something had to be wrong.

"Is something bothering your back?" she asked as she toed off her ankle boots.

He looked at her and smiled. "Yeah, my wings itch."

"Uh, wings? How did I not know you had wings?"

"I'm a cupid, and I don't know why I didn't mention it, other than I've only had them out of my back once. I knocked over everything in my living room. Scared Brayden a bit, I think."

"Can I seem them?"

Tyler with wings. That could be hot.

He grinned and took off his cable knit sweater, and Abby just about swallowed her tongue.

Oh. My. God.

She loved the way he looked. Those

lickable abs had to have at least eight little sections made for her touch. His hard chest made him look manly, and not like he had bigger boobs than most women.

She held back a snort at that thought.

But her favorite part? The V-lines that led to below his jeans. Oh, yes, she couldn't wait to lick those and see where those and the happy trail of fine hair he had led to.

Tonight.

He wouldn't be able to put her off for long because she had to taste him. Soon.

"Holy fuck, I love when you look at me like that."

"Like what?"

"Like you want to taste every inch of me and take my cock deep down your throat."

Her pussy ached at his words. "I'm going to, you know. Tonight."

His body shuddered, and he licked his lips.

Well, that was different. Who knew she could almost come by just *looking* at a man licking his lips?

She held on to the back of her couch for support. No use falling and breaking something when she had her man right in front of her.

Abby watched as wings sprouted from his back, and he grunted.

"It hurts, Ty? Don't do it if it hurts." She ran up to him and put her hands on his chest, the heat radiating from him almost scalding.

"It hurts if I don't do it. I've been hiding them for too long."

He winced then let out a breath, and she looked at his pink wings.

She snorted. "Pink?"

Tyler growled and pulled her in for a bruising kiss. "They're white with a little bit of an accent. If you think they're too pink, I'll show you what I can do. Think I'm too pink to be manly?" He ended his promise with a thrust toward her, his cock hard and ready beneath his jeans.

She smiled up at him then sank to her knees.

"Abby?"

"Shh, I'm going to taste you since you didn't let me before." She traced her fingers down those lines on his hips and watched his body shake.

"Can't say that I'm going to argue with you," he said then gritted his teeth as she undid his jeans.

"Commando? Really?" she asked as his thick cock sprang from the confines of his jeans and she gripped it.

She'd never held one before, but she was pretty sure he had to be bigger than others. She couldn't even wrap her hand all the way around it. How on earth did he fit in her?

Memories of how tightly he did filled her mind, and she creamed right there.

"God, I love the way you look on your knees, your face all flushed, and my dick in your hands."

She smiled then licked the head, the salty taste exploding on her tongue.

"Shit," he grunted then wrapped his hand in her hair.

Abby let her tongue tease his slit, and

then she licked up the vein underneath. She'd seen enough porn to know how to give a blowjob, but she wanted to take her time.

She licked him up like an ice cream cone then sucked on the head, letting her tongue swirl around the crown.

His fist tightened, and she looked up at him.

"Shit, your eyes are so big and dark when you look up at me like that. You want to go deeper?"

She nodded around him then looked down at her treat as she swallowed a bit more, his cock fully in her mouth. She breathed through her nose but still gagged a bit as he hit the back of her throat.

"Shit, baby, sorry," he said as he tugged on her hair to pull her back.

The slight sting as he did it went all the way to her core, and she gripped his hips to keep him where he was. She looked up at him and swallowed more, this time relaxing her throat so she could take more of him.

"Abigail," he whispered, and she was pretty sure her eyes crossed.

She took him deeper a few more times then pulled back so she could suck on the crown and lick up the sides. She wrapped one hand around the base so she could add more grip and sucked harder. He thrust in and out of her mouth, one hand on the couch, the other in her hair. With her other hand, she cupped his balls, rolling them and using her fingers to massage the skin behind them.

When his dick started to throb, she hollowed her cheeks, and he shouted her name as his salty cum splashed on her tongue. She didn't let go but flattened her tongue so she could swallow it all.

When she pulled back, she looked up at him and smiled. She was pretty sure she'd drenched her panties just by tasting him. Who knew her Tyler was an aphrodisiac?

"Holy shit, baby. That's the hottest thing I've ever seen. Who knew my Abby was such a dirty girl?"

"I've always wanted to do that."

"You told me you watched porn, and now I'm glad you did." She watched as his wings flexed as he brought them into his back. "Don't move. I'm not done with you."

She swallowed hard as he went to the bedroom naked then came back with her wand in his hand.

"Tyler?"

"You told me you liked to play, so that's what we're doing. You like clit stimulation, right?"

She nodded, unable to talk.

He turned on the cordless wand, and it vibrated in his hand. "This is gonna be fun. Take off your dress. Slowly." He palmed his still-hard cock and smiled.

A shudder ripped through her, and she unzipped the back of her dress then slowly stepped out of it, each movement brushing against her too-sensitive skin.

She stood in her black panties, bra, and matching thigh-high stockings and shivered.

"Dear God, woman. You were wearing those underneath your dress all night?"

She smiled and nodded. "I wanted to surprise you."

He kissed her softly. "I'm the luckiest guy ever."

"Really?"

"Really. Now, I'm going to take off your panties and bra, but keep the thigh-high stockings on. Okay?"

She nodded, ready for him to touch her.

He slowly undid her bra, and her breasts fell heavy, wanting. He blew cold air on each of her nipples, and she moaned. The coolness on her too-hot skin made her want to come.

Now.

She desperately wanted him to suck her or at least touch her, but he got on his knees and took off her panties, purposely not touching her skin.

Bastard.

"Tyler…"

"I'm going to touch you, Abigail. Just let me look at you first."

"Meanie."

"You say that to a man who's about to let you come?"

"Fine."

He threw his head back and laughed. "I love you."

"Love you, too," she said as he nudged her knees apart.

He picked up the vibrator and rolled it up her legs, the vibrations going directly to her core.

"I love the way you respond, baby. You're mine."

"As long as you know you're mine, too."

"Deal," he said then brushed the wand on her clit.

She gripped the back of the couch, her ass resting on the side of it so Tyler was supporting her weight. Her legs spread around Tyler's shoulders and her head dipped back. He rolled it over her, increasing the speed as he did so, then inserted two fingers, curling them so he could hit her in the spot that made her scream.

Before he could add another finger, or do whatever he'd planned next, she came. Hard. Her knees gave out as her body vibrated, flushed and numbed. She felt Tyler's hand on her as she came down, her legs wrapped around him.

"That was so fucking beautiful," he said as he kissed her softly, kneading her breasts as he did so.

"I don't think I can stand up," she said.

"You'll have to because I'm going to bend you over this couch and fuck you hard."

"Oh, God," she whispered.

"No, my name is Tyler."

She rolled her eyes and stood on shaky legs as he turned her around and bent her over the couch. He ran his hands down her back, her sides, cupping her ass as he licked her neck, kissing her where he could.

She heard the sound of a foil wrapper then felt the head of his cock at her pussy, throbbing and ready. She leaned back and smiled as he cursed.

"That's right, take me in," he grunted and pushed forward harder until she felt his hips against her ass.

Oh, God, they were connected in every way possible. As sappy as that sounded, it still brought tears to her eyes.

Tyler pulled back, gripped her hips, and plunged again and again, each time a little bit harder, a little bit deeper.

She closed her eyes, relishing the feel of him filling her, and she felt her back tingle, her legs go numb, and her inner walls tighten as she came again, this time Tyler coming with her as she felt his seed fill the condom.

"We have to do that again," she whispered, unable to speak any louder.

"Any time, love, any time."

That sounded like the best plan ever. Nothing could change the way she felt this moment. Nothing.

Chapter 11

Abby bent over in her jeans and looked at her ass in the mirror.

Good, no butt crack.

Even though her dancing jeans were hip-hugging tight, that didn't mean she wanted to show the world her ass. Plus, she wasn't sure

Tyler would appreciate that. Not that he wouldn't enjoy her in tight jeans. It was more that he might not care for the whole everyone-else-looking-at-her-thing. For some reason she really liked his possessive attitude.

She wiggled her hips as she bent over, making sure there wouldn't be any unwelcome surprises later at the dance and heard a groan.

"Fuck, Abigail, what are you doing?" Tyler said from the doorway.

Still bent over, she laughed as she looked through her legs. For some reason, she really wanted to tease him. Bending over in the tightest jeans she owned, pretty sure he'd never seen them before, was the best way to do that.

He stalked toward her, his gaze darkening with each step, then stopped behind her. She shivered as he palmed her cheek, rubbing her through her jeans.

"I like these," he whispered, his voice hoarse.

She smiled then wiggled again, leaning into his erection.

"Jesus, okay, we need to stop. I promised you a date at the town Valentine's

Day dance, and if you stay bent over like this, I'm going to strip you of these jeans and fuck you right here in front of the mirror."

She gasped and wiggled again. He gripped her hips hard, stalling her movement.

"You like that idea? Us in front of a mirror as I slam into that pretty pussy?"

She nodded, eager. Who cared about a silly dance anyway?

"I thought you might." He reached down to her stomach and pulled her up so she was standing flush against him. "But I'm going to take you to that dance. I know you've always wanted to go with someone, and I'm not taking that away from you, got it?'

She turned in his hold, even as happiness slid through her like butter. "You really are a good man, Tyler Cooper."

He traced her jaw with his finger and smiled. "Don't let the town know that. I'm supposed to be the hard-assed sheriff who doesn't bow down to anyone."

She stood on her tiptoes and kissed his chin. "It'll be our secret."

"Tell me about these jeans, Abigail. I knew you were a dirtier girl than you let on, but these? Fuck, they're perfect for that ass of yours."

Abby let out a laugh and shook her head. "These are my dancing clothes. I usually wear them when I go to the dance hall in Larimer County, but I thought I'd wear them out with you tonight since the dance is casual."

"I'm glad you did, baby. You look amazing, plus I get to show you off so the town will know what they were missing."

She shook her head and wrapped her arms around him. "I don't need to prove myself to them, Tyler. I never did. Not really."

"I know that, but it's still fun to show you off."

She rolled her eyes and led him to their coats and then to his SUV. Even though it wasn't Valentine's Day yet, the town liked to hold their annual dance to showcase the love of some of their couples. Really, it was just so the old busybodies could gossip like schoolgirls as to who was dating who, but Abby would take it. She'd never been to the dance with a date before.

Even though she'd been looking forward to the dance, as they pulled up to the gym, those butterflies in her stomach started flapping full force.

She'd seen how the women in town treated her already without her putting herself on display. Yet now she was going into the lion's den, complete with tight jeans and Tyler on her arm. What the hell had she been thinking? She'd already had to deal with the whispers, and the not-so-quiet taunts, the stares, and the attitudes. Why was she subjecting herself to this?

"Abigail? We don't hide. We don't have to. What we have is good, okay, baby? Don't beat yourself up."

"How do you know what I'm thinking?"

He turned in his seat as he cut the engine. "Because I know you. I've always known you, even if I didn't know it."

Abby burst out laughing. "Oh, my God, that's the most convoluted thing you've ever said, but I still love you for it. We're going to be fine. I'm just not in the mood to deal with attitude."

"You know between my brothers and I,

we won't let them hurt you."

"I need to stand up for myself you know."

"And you have been. I've seen the way you stand tall and don't take shit from people like Clara. You're amazing."

"Well, I just hope I keep my harpiness at bay because I'm not in the mood to find out what other changes are in store for me in public, you know?"

Tyler frowned then kissed her forehead, a soft touch of lips that conveyed more emotion than she'd even known possible.

"I don't know what's going to happen, but we'll take it as it comes. I kind of like how possessive you get sometimes though. It's hot."

Abby rolled her eyes. "Really? Because I'm pretty sure all the women you've *dated* in the past have been possessive in some way or another, and I bet you weren't thrilled about that."

Tyler grinned, and Abby fell in love with that smile...again. "True. But you're my Abigail. You're allowed to fight off women who want to attack little old me."

She laughed but wanted to scream in joy at his "my Abigail" remark.

Who knew Tyler Cooper was such a softie?

Well, considering he was a cupid, it sort of made sense.

They walked into the gym, and she felt every eye on her. Every single one. Why was it so weird that she was with a date? Okay, fine, so she'd never been on one. Whatever. Maybe they were looking at Tyler and wondering what he was doing with her. Maybe it was a combination of both.

Why had she done this again?

Tyler cleared his throat and slowly let his gaze rest on everyone in the gym. People fidgeted and got back to dancing or talking.

Man, that was sexy.

"You okay?" he whispered.

"I'm fine. But I kind of like the whole alpha thing you just did."

Tyler laughed. "Let's go dance. I want to see how you move in those jeans."

Abby raised a brow. "Really? You're going to objectify me like that?" she teased.

"Damn straight," he growled against her ear. "Then I'm going to peel them off later and make sure I get to know each curve. Again."

She shivered and let him lead her to the dance floor. It was late enough that the kids were gone. Only adults remained at the dance, and the couples on the dance floor ranged from sweet to a bit raunchy. Abby knew she could have played it sweet and danced like she knew the town expected of her, at least as they had before she started dating Tyler. But tonight she wanted to be herself.

Abby wrapped her arms around Tyler's waist, swaying her ample hips from side to side, and watched as Tyler's pupils dilated and his breath caught.

"Damn, I knew you'd look good dancing in those jeans."

She smiled, practically purring. "Only for you." She swiveled, and she heard him groan.

They danced like they were the only two in the room but kept it relatively clean considering where they were.

God, she loved this man.

The next song came on, a slower one, and Tyler framed her face with his hands. "Another dance?"

"Yes, please," she breathed.

He held their clasped hands to his chest and wrapped the other arm around her as they swayed to the music.

Okay, so this could make up for the past. It had to. No magic involved, just them acting like they should. She could have made him get on his knees and beg for forgiveness, but what was there to forgive? It was Aeneas's fault that Tyler hadn't been able to find his true feelings for her. It had been Aeneas who had kidnapped her and turned her into a harpy.

It wasn't Tyler.

"Hey, what's with the frown?" Tyler asked as he kissed her nose. "Did I step on your toes?"

"No, I was just thinking about how far we've come."

He smiled and kissed her softly. "And look how far we can go."

"You couldn't do any better than that, Tyler?" Mrs. Ellis, the cranky old woman who seemed to hate everything about Abby, walked toward them.

The old woman's blonde wig was askew like usual, her makeup too bright, and her eyes filled with anger.

Tyler slowly straightened and turned toward Mrs. Ellis. He gripped Abby's hand and squeezed.

"I'm not sure what you're talking about, ma'am, but I'd be sure to watch my tongue if I were you," he drawled, every bit the sheriff.

That sense of anger and protectiveness that Abby hadn't felt before the arrow had struck filled her belly and spread throughout her body. Who did this woman think she was? Abby clenched her fists, the skin breaking as her newly formed talons cut into her palms.

"Tyler, dear, I don't know why you're shacking up with this one, but you could do better. Maybe Abigail likes to be on her back, but you could find a real relationship with a woman who's her better. One who is on your level. Ignore this one, dear, and find someone better suited."

"You need to go now, Mrs. Ellis," Abby said, her voice deepening with the rage that swarmed through her.

She felt more than saw the other Coopers coming to surround her with protection as the gym quieted. Matt and Jordan stood behind her, Jordan's hand on Abby's shoulder. Rina and Justin stood on Tyler's side Jackson and Brayden came up beside Abby, scowls on their faces.

Warmth spread through her at the thought of this family standing beside her, making her feel as though she was a part of them.

Tyler narrowed his eyes and curled his lip. "You and all your little busybody friends can go to hell. I don't know what the fuck your problem is with Abigail, but you need to get the fuck over it. Do you understand me? Abigail is the best of everything, the best of goodness. She's watched your children, she's helped with every event in town, she's done everything for you."

He took a breath, and Abby stood there in awe of the man who would stand up for her.

"Don't you fucking open your mouth,

Mrs. Ellis," he continued, and the old lady gasped again at his language. "I'm so tired of the way you look down on Abigail and the Coopers until you need something. Abigail had done nothing to deserve anything you've done. Anything anyone of you have done," he said to the crowd gathered around them.

"I love this woman. Why can't you understand that? I'm not stepping down to be with her. No, she's the one who had to do that for me."

"That's not true, Ty," she whispered.

He smiled at her and cupped her chin. "I love you, Abigail. You, just you, and everything about you."

"I love you, too, Tyler."

"Touching, but it doesn't change anything. You're too good for her, Tyler Cooper," Mrs. Ellis spat.

Tyler looked at Mrs. Ellis like she'd gone crazy. Considering the woman looked down on the Coopers as well, Abby wasn't sure she wanted to know where she ranked in the scheme of things—nor did she care.

"I'm sorry you think that, Mrs. Ellis,"

Abby said, surprised there wasn't more rage in her voice. She was just tired of it all. She didn't want to defend her relationship anymore. She had Tyler and the Coopers. She didn't need anyone else. "But, you don't get to decide anything about my life. Now just go away."

"And be sure you don't drive," Tyler added in, and the other woman snarled as she stomped away.

The crowd dispersed as the drama ended, and Abby hugged the man she loved.

"Thanks for standing up for me," she whispered into his chest.

"I shouldn't have to do that."

"You can't help the way people see things. All you can do is live your life and make the best of it."

He kissed her and led her toward the exit. "I still don't like it."

She waved at Matt and Jordan as they walked to their car with Rina and Justin. Brayden and Jackson got in another car and nodded toward them.

These people were her family.

Not the ones who made her feel like nothing.

"We're all going over to Jackson's house for drinks, right?" Abby asked as they got into Tyler's SUV.

"If you still want to. I know this night didn't turn out like we wanted. I'm sorry, baby."

"Hey, stop that. You didn't do anything wrong. I think though that things will be different. Did you notice that people had nothing to say after you stood up for me? I think they're finally getting over it. And frankly, it was just the women in town acting like jealous shrews."

Tyler laughed and started toward Jackson's. "Tell me how you really feel."

"Well, if you hadn't been such a man-whore, we wouldn't have that problem," she teased.

"Ouch, you wound me. And you know I wasn't that bad."

"You kind of were, but you're better now. Right?" She narrowed her gaze, and he laughed.

"I promise, baby. I'm reformed."

"Uh-huh. We'll just have to make sure."

"Oh, really, how are you going to do that?"

"Well, I was thinking along the lines of a blowjob that will make you forget everything else."

The car swerved, and Abby laughed. "Don't do that to me when I'm driving, Abigail."

"Sorry."

"No you're not."

"True."

"Shit!" Tyler yelled as he slammed on the brakes.

Abby braced herself as he pulled to a stop, and she looked out the window.

Aeneas stood in the middle of the road, a smile on his face.

Visions of what he'd done to her assaulted her. The scars that still lined her body burned in protest, and her heartbeat sped.

"Stay in the car, Abigail," Tyler said as he got out.

"What? No, don't do this. I can help you."

He leaned over and kissed her hard. "I can't think if you're in danger, okay? Stay here and get in the driver's seat so you can drive away if you need to."

"Not without you."

"Please, Abigail."

"Fine, but if you get hurt, I'm going to kick your ass. He's not worth it, Tyler."

"I love you."

"I love you, too. Be careful."

She climbed into the driver's seat and watched as the love of her life walked toward Aeneas. She rolled down the window so she could hear.

"What you are doing, Aeneas? You lost? Go home," Tyler said calmly. More calmly than she would have spoken.

"I see you're still with her. For now."

"Forever, if I have any say in it."

Forever? She'd have to put that aside for now.

"I haven't lost yet. I'll just have to change my plans."

"Just leave us. You can't win."

"I didn't get to keep my Dido, so you can't keep your Abigail."

"Dido?" Tyler asked, echoing Abigail's thoughts.

"My love. She was the first of Cupid's follies. The first to be struck by an arrow. Because of that, she's gone. Why can't you understand that?"

All of this because Dido, the woman Aeneas had loved, was gone? But what did that mean? Had she died? Had she left him? What did this have to do with Cupid? They'd looked up the history, but they'd never thought, even with the rare name, it had been the same person. Plus, it hadn't made sense to them that Aeneas's vengeance would last so long. There were way too many questions and not enough answers. She gripped the steering wheel.

Come on, Tyler, don't do anything stupid.

Like get out of the freaking car when a crazy man stood outside.

"The histories said that you left Dido," Tyler said, and Abby winced.

Antagonizing the man is not the best thing to do, Tyler.

"The histories have it wrong," Aeneas spat. "I didn't leave her. Not really. She died because of Cupid."

Unable to watch anymore, Abby got out of the car, ignoring Tyler's scowl.

"I'm sorry, Aeneas, that she died. She must have loved you," she said, taking a guess.

"Of course she did! We were in love before the first strike of an arrow. But Cupid had to ruin it all. All that magic was too much for her and she couldn't stay with me. And because of that pain, I was doomed to roam the earth without her for eternity. But at least I'm not human...or a cupid."

"I'm sorry you lost her."

"She killed herself because of Cupid and his magic. But, I won't let her die in vain. Watch yourselves because I'll find a way to make you lose everything you want."

With that, he shot forward, faster than she would have thought possible, threw Tyler across the hood of the SUV and Tyler landed with a grunt, and had Abby in his hands by the neck.

She struggled in his hold, the harpy in her coming out, her talons scraping against his skin.

"I won't kill you, not now, but be warned: I will make you, your man, and all the other cupids pay." He squeezed harder, and black spots formed behind her eyes. He dropped her, and she fell to her knees, a sharp pain radiating through her legs.

Before she could open her eyes, he was gone and Tyler was by her side.

"Abigail? Baby? Talk to me."

"I'm fine," she croaked out.

"Why did you get out of the car?" he asked as he got them in the SUV and on their way to Jackson's.

"I didn't want you to stand alone."

"I'm never alone, not anymore."

"He's not done with us, is he?" she asked as they pulled up to Jackson's. Even though Apneas had already said that very thing, she needed to hear it from Tyler.

"No, so I don't want you to go out alone."

"You're not allowed to either." She held up her hand. "Don't pull that tough guy crap."

"Fine, but we'll find a way to stop him."

"I could use that drink now."

"Good, because Jackson is staring at us from the porch and looks angry. You'd think this was an actual event, not just a get-together. My brother is a bit crazy about being late."

"What's new about that?" she asked as Tyler laughed.

It was good to see him laugh because she knew it wasn't over with Aeneas. Not by a long shot.

Chapter 12

"We're going to have to figure out how to take care of this guy," Jackson said as he took another drink of his beer.

Tyler nodded and did the same. "He's seriously crazy, Jacks."

"All of this because of a woman that he

left?" Brayden asked, a frown on his face.

Tyler nodded. "I remember reading something about Dido and Aeneas and how they were the first couple Cupid introduced through his arrow. But I never thought it was the same Aeneas. I didn't think he could live that long. But I should have considering how old Santa is."

"The man wants to deny cupids love because he left the one he loved and changed his mind?" Jackson said as he scowled. "He's an idiot."

"Tell it like it is, Jacks," Brayden drawled. "Well, we can't let you and Abby out of our sights. There's no way we're letting the two of you alone."

"I can take care of Abigail," Tyler said, even as the doubt crept in.

He'd seen the way Aeneas had taken over in a matter of moments. Tyler hadn't even had time to figure out how to use his new cupid strength to defend himself, let alone Abigail. Cupids shouldn't have needed strength to do their job, but Tyler liked the extra perk anyway. He'd watched from the hood of the SUV, trying to get up, as Abigail clawed at Aeneas with her talons, yet he couldn't break free of his hold.

They'd have to find a way, other than brute strength, to defeat the man. There was no way they could live the rest of their lives on guard, always afraid of where to turn because of a crazy man with a death wish. He wanted to raise babies with his Abigail and watch them grow up safe and sound. He wanted to grow old with Abigail and live long and happy lives together.

They wouldn't be able to do that with Aeneas around.

And, yes, before all this, all those thoughts would have sent him into a crazy spin of bachelor attitude, but not anymore.

He wanted Abigail in his life forever.

As soon as they took care of Aeneas, he'd ask her to marry him.

They might have been together only a couple weeks, but their relationship was different. They'd loved each other for years, yet Tyler hadn't known it. The feelings the he had were those of years of love, not just the moments he felt now. He didn't want to waste any more time.

He just had to make sure they would be safe first.

Easier said than done.

"Tyler?" Jackson asked. "Are you listening?"

He shook his head to clear his thoughts. There would be more than enough time to think of his future with Abigail once they found a way to stop Aeneas.

"Sorry, no, I wasn't," he finally said. "What were you saying?"

Jackson raised a brow but didn't comment on Tyler's lack of attention. Sometimes his brother was a little too much like a parent.

"We were just trying to plan how to keep you safe. Any thoughts?"

Tyler let out a breath. "Sorry again. And I'm not sure. I know we don't want Abigail to be alone; that's a given."

"Of course," Brayden said. "I don't think any of us should be alone either. Just in case he tries to go after more of the family."

"Okay, we need to call Ally then and let

her know."

Brayden's eyes stormed over when they mentioned Ally's name. "I already thought that. I'll go to her place and let her know."

"And drive alone?" Jackson asked.

"You can come with me if you want, but I don't want her alone with the kids."

How on earth did Brayden not know he was in love with the woman?

"Okay," Jackson said and stood up. "The rest of you guys can stay here for a while. We'll call and then figure out what to do for the future. At least for now though, I'd like to keep everyone safe in groups."

"Are you okay to drive?" Tyler asked.

Both brothers nodded.

"Only had half of mine," Brayden said. He gave Tyler a brief hug and walked out, Jackson following behind.

Aeneas had them all worried; yet there was nothing Tyler could think of to stop the man, or whatever he was.

"Tyler?" Abigail asked as she sat beside

him on the couch.

"I'm fine. Brayden and Jackson just left to take care of Ally and the kids."

She bit her lip and leaned into him. "We put them in danger, didn't we?"

He hugged her tight and kissed her temple. "No, never think that. Aeneas is the one who did. Not you. Not me."

"But if it weren't for us..."

"No, stop it." He gripped her chin and forced her gaze to his. "Aeneas is the one who left Dido and lost her. She killed herself. Cupid didn't kill her."

She cupped his cheek and tilted her head. She cupped his cheek and tilted her head. "I know that. Cupid's magic, *your* magic, isn't the reason these things happen. Your magic is love, not pain. You don't force people to fall for each other. You just take down that internal barrier. You can't do wrong with your magic, Ty."

Some of the tension eased out of his shoulders at her words. "How on earth did you know what I was thinking before I even realized it?"

"Because I know you. You're worried that you'll somehow cause something like this in the future. You care about people, Tyler, even when the curse was on you. You're the sheriff. You take care of everyone you can. You don't want to think about the idea that you could somehow hurt someone with your powers."

Yes, he'd been worried, but he'd never voiced it. Even though he knew that Aeneas was the one who had caused everything, there was still that lingering doubt.

"I just don't want to cause that same pain."

"You can't, Tyler. Aeneas left Dido for his own reasons, but Cupid had nothing to do with it. Just because the arrow takes away that barrier doesn't mean they'll be together forever. Not that I know a lot about them, but I do know that relationships take work. They're not just happiness and rainbows. They take time, effort, energy, and everything in between."

"I'm not the best person at relationships either, you know."

"I do know. That's why we're going to

work hard together at it. We don't just get to leave when things get tough."

He touched his forehead to hers. "We need to beat him."

"I know. But how?"

"We can't win against his strength. I don't know how to use mine all the time. I'm not reliable."

"And I don't even know what I have yet. I mean it looks like only a temper and talons. Not that much help in the long run."

He kissed her nose and inhaled her sweet rose scent. "Then we'll find another way."

"How?" she asked again.

"Okay, what do we have that can hurt him?"

"What about your arrows?"

He shook his head. "No, that won't do it. It only finds the one that he loves, right? Well, Dido is long since gone."

Arrows...

"What about *his* arrows?" he asked as an

idea formed in his mind.

"What do you mean?" Abigail asked, even as her eyes widened as her thoughts seemed to be similar to his own.

"His arrows. They take away the one thing that makes a person themselves. They took our possibilities." He growled at that and tugged her closer, needed to feel her warmth. "And when he hit you with it, he tried to take your kindness. But I think he made a mistake there since you're stronger than he is."

She grinned. "I'm not the same person I was, but I can control my anger if I think of you. But what would hitting him with his own arrow do?"

"I don't know exactly. But it might help. What makes him, *him*?"

"His anger? His loss? His immortality? Pretty much everything."

He nodded. "Any of those would work. Maybe it will take away something to make it easier for us to take him down and keep you safe."

"How are we going to get them though?"

"Well, he always has them on him. He has to. They're a part of him."

"He's more like a cupid than he wants to admit."

"Maybe it will turn him into a cupid. Though with the way he likes to cause pain, I'm not sure I want him to have anything to do with love."

Anger coursed through him at the memory of Abigail in the dark room, blood surrounding her as she writhed in pain.

Oh, he'd kill the man if he could just for that.

"I'm okay," she whispered. "Stop thinking of what happened."

Easier said than done.

"You first," he said as he watched the shadows in her eyes dance.

"We're not going to figure it out right now. Let's just rest so we have the energy to take him," she said as she laid her head on his chest.

He caressed her thigh through her tight jeans and sighed. There wasn't a way to make everything better with just a wish. They had no idea where Aeneas lived or stayed when he was in town. The only thing they could do was prepare to take him down with his own arrow when the time came.

With Jackson and Brayden at Ally's to protect her and the kids, Tyler felt somewhat better. That left him, Justin, and Matt to stay with Rina, Abigail, and Jordan. Though Justin and Rina have a connection in which they could use magic, he didn't know if it would be enough to take down Aeneas. And Jordan could use her magic to protect what she could.

Together, they had a chance.

He'd just closed his eyes to rest for a moment when the first smell of smoke reached him.

He opened his eyes and cursed. Smoke filled the house, and he pulled Abigail into his arms and ran out the door, yelling to his brothers as he did so.

Abby woke at the first touch and startled. "What, Tyler?"

He put her down and watched as the rest of his family ran out the house behind him, coats in their hands. Thank God his family thought of things like that. He'd only been thinking of Abigail and getting her out of there.

"What's going on?" Jordan asked as they pulled on their coats.

"Where's the fire?" Matt asked as they all looked around.

"Is this Aeneas?" Justin asked.

Tyler didn't know for sure, but he thought it had to be. Something didn't feel right.

"Over there!" Rina called out and pointed to the ridge across the large field.

"Oh, hell, the fire wasn't in the house; it's in the field," Tyler said as he ran a hand through his hair.

"But there's snow on the ground. How is the fire spreading like that, and why is there so much smoke in the house?" Abigail asked as she gripped his hand.

"Because it's not a normal fire," Jordan said as she anxiously cracked her knuckles. Sparks of magic flowed off of them with the movement. "It's magic. We're not going to be able to stop it with water. I might be able to stop it from spreading if I have Matt's help with his energy."

"Rina and I can get the other end," Justin said, and he gripped Rina's hand.

"But we can't put it completely out if Aeneas is there to keep adding onto the flames."

Tyler nodded, purpose setting in. "Then Abigail and I are going to have to find him and his arrows."

"Arrows?" Matt asked.

"If we hit him with his own arrow—" Tyler began.

"You can take away something from him and hopefully stop him," Jordan finished, a smile on her face. "Nice. Okay, we have a plan."

"I just texted Jackson to keep everyone at Ally's house. No use adding more people who can't help because they don't have magic."

"At least not yet," Rina said. She waved her hand at the questions on their faces. "So not the time. Come on, we have a crazy non-Cupid guy to take down."

Tyler nodded then turned to Abigail. "I'd

rather you were safe at Ally's." She opened her mouth to protest, but he cut her off. "But I know you'd only come back. That's why I want you by my side where I can keep you safe."

"And I can keep you safe as well."

He kissed her hard; trying to let her know every emotion and feel every ounce of love he had for her. He pulled away, both of them panting.

"We'll finish that later?" she asked.

"Deal."

The six of them ran toward the ridge as the smoke flowed around them and the flames got bigger. God, he didn't want to put his family in danger, but Aeneas wouldn't stop unless they took him down.

"It's about time you got here," Aeneas called from the tree line, near the fire.

Of course the bastard wouldn't want to be hurt by flames.

Rina, Justin, Matt, and Jordan ran off to deal with the flames, and Abigail gripped his hand as the faced off against Aeneas.

They would fight, and they would win.

Together.

They had to.

"We got your call. Now stop this and leave."

"If I can't make you lose the one you love through your own actions, I'll make sure you lose her when my fire touches her."

He squeezed Abigail's hand. There was no way in hell he'd let her leave him.

He looked around Aeneas, trying to see what the man had on him, but he didn't see the arrows. That didn't mean they didn't exist though. Abigail had said she'd seen them in the room before she'd been shot with one meaning they weren't like his own, invisible unless in the presence of their true love or another...whatever Aeneas was.

The arrows would be around him somewhere. The man couldn't afford to be without them.

Of this, Tyler was sure.

He leaned down to Abigail and whispered in her ear, "I'll distract him. You find his arrows. They need to be here. Try looking in that copse of trees."

She nodded, never removing her gaze from Aeneas.

Tyler let go of her hand, even though he never wanted to leave her side.

"You can't break us, Aeneas."

"I can, and I will."

Aeneas came at him, venom in his glare. Tyler braced himself and pulled deep on that newfound energy and strength. The other man pushed at him, and Tyler ducked, knocking the man in the head with his arm. Aeneas shifted, reaching out to punch him.

Tyler ducked again, but too slow, and winced as the other man's fist connected with his jaw. But he didn't stop; he couldn't stop.

He lashed out, clipping Aeneas in the cheek, and the other man punched, throwing Tyler to the ground.

They wrestled, each equal in weight and strength.

At least for now.

Tyler didn't want to think about what

would happen if he suddenly lost the strength he had.

"I'm going to kill you for what happened to Dido," Aeneas screamed.

Apparently, Aeneas didn't want just Abigail to suffer anymore.

"She killed herself. We didn't hurt her."

"But you did. All you fucking cupids did."

Tyler tried to slam Aeneas's head into the ground, but the other man rolled and kicked him. They fought harder, punching, kicking, but not getting anywhere.

He hoped to God that Abigail could find that arrow.

Aeneas pulled back and smiled then moved faster than Tyler thought he could. He heard a scream as Aeneas gripped Abigail by the arm and tossed her into the flames, her voice fracturing as the fire burned her.

A shot of magic hurled in the air as Jordan slapped Aeneas with a lick of flame. The other man screamed in agony as Tyler hurried past him.

"Abigail!" Tyler ran toward where she lay on the ground, the flames around her licking, burning. She stood but almost fell into the flames again.

Tyler pulled her out, setting her on the snow.

"Oh, God, baby."

Burns covered her arms and legs, but nowhere else since her clothes were fine elsewhere. They didn't look to be past first or second, and he knew her new healing abilities would help, but he didn't know if it would be enough.

"I'm fine. It doesn't hurt that bad," she said as she winced.

He kissed her forehead. Tears were running down both their cheeks. "I'll finish him."

A hand gripped his collar and pulled him back. He fell to the ground with a wince. Aeneas stood over him, a smile on his face.

"Your darling is in pain. Good. She won't die. Not yet. I want her to watch me kill you. I don't care which one dies, as long as the other lives to feel pain."

Aeneas struck out, punching over and over again. Tyler covered his face and tried to get away, but the other man was faster.

He rolled to the side, grunting as a fist connected with his kidneys, and kicked out.

Aeneas fell to the ground, and Tyler punched again.

Okay, this was getting old.

Tyler reached out, grabbed the other man by the shoulders, and rolled, flipping Aeneas onto his back. Aeneas kicked, and they rolled again, this time with Aeneas landing on top.

The other man wrapped his hands around Tyler's neck and squeezed. Tyler tried to claw at him, but it didn't work. He couldn't break free.

His vision blurred as he struggled to breathe.

Oh, God, this couldn't be it.

He couldn't die. Not now. Not when he'd just found his Abigail.

Aeneas grunted, his eyes wide, then he screamed in pain.

Tyler quickly pushed the bastard off and stood over him. He looked to where Abigail stood on shaky legs, a bow in her hand, and a sad smile on her face.

"Found it," she whispered.

Tyler left Aeneas where he writhed in agony on the snow. He felt more than saw the flames die down and the rest of his family run to his side.

But he had eyes for only Abigail.

He cupped her cheeks and kissed her softly, not wanting to hurt her, even though he wanted to take her in every primal way to make sure she was okay and to prove that she was his.

"I'm okay," she whispered, and he shook his head.

"You're burned," he rasped out.

"I'm already healing."

"I'm going to take care of you."

"You already are."

"Nice shot!" Justin said as he kicked Aeneas in the side when the bastard tried to stand up.

Abigail gave a pained smile. "Thanks."

Even though his body hurt like hell and he was pretty sure every part of him had a bruise, Tyler picked her up and held her close to his chest.

"How is everyone else?" he asked as he took a good look at all of them. They all looked worse for wear with slight burns and sooty faces but otherwise looked healthy.

"Good," Matt said as he glared at the man on the ground. "Now what are we going to do with you?"

Jordan narrowed her eyes then grinned. "You're human now. You know I'm a witch and can tell these things. Well, how about that?"

Rina shook her head. "The one thing you didn't want to be. Powerless."

Tyler set Abigail on her feet and leaned over the man who had almost cost him everything.

"I'm not going to kill you. No, I'm going to make you live this way until you die. Which will happen. You're not immortal anymore.

You're human now."

Aeneas glared. "I'll find a way to come back for you."

Abigail shook her head and spoke softly. "Just quit already. She can't come back. But if you move on and try to live your life without the pain in your heart, maybe you can live again."

That was a much nicer way of saying what thoughts Tyler had in his head, but he wouldn't disagree with her.

"Stay away from us and you're safe," Tyler said. "If you come near me or my family again, I'll kill you. Make no mistake by our actions here that we're weak."

Aeneas tried to get up, but the Coopers pushed him down. Finally, the man nodded, defeated.

"I don't have my magic anymore," he whispered. "It's done."

Tyler nodded. "Then leave. We don't want you here."

They let the man get up and stumble away. In the distance Tyler saw Jackson pull up, and Tyler nodded toward him.

"Make sure he get's out of town," Tyler yelled.

Jackson nodded and walked toward the beaten man.

His brother would make sure the bastard would leave town.

He lifted Abigail in his arms and inhaled her rose scent that was now laced with smoke.

"Let me take care of you."

"It's over, isn't it?"

"Well, we're just beginning."

Matt groaned, and Justin laughed behind him.

"Smooth," Abigail said as she kissed him.

With her soft lips beneath his, he could do anything. And now it looked as if they had a future, so they could plan it.

Chapter 13

"Happy Valentine's Day," Tyler whispered into Abby's ear as he rolled his hips against her.

She smiled, utterly content, if not a bit sore. They'd slept the entire day before, not caring that they probably had work to do. Jackson had left a note saying Aeneas had left town, and for some reason, Abigail felt confident that they were safe from the man who'd lost his powers.

Tyler had bandaged her burns, and she had soothed his bruises. They hadn't made love, though she knew they'd both wanted to. But sometimes those aches and pains were a little too much to get in the mood.

It seemed so surreal that they were in her home, in her bed, wrapped naked around each other. It had been only two weeks since she'd cut Tyler with the arrow and her life had changed forever.

Now she knew he loved her, even though she'd loved him for much longer. Now she wasn't moving, and she'd have her job back in the fall if she wanted it. She was part of the Coopers in every way possible except for her name, and she loved it.

Aeneas had tried to kill them, keep them apart, and break them, but it was all over. He wouldn't be hurting them, not anymore. Now they could find their own way through their relationship and figure out how to love each other and grow together.

A scary thing for a girl who had never

had a boyfriend before.

Tyler Cooper was her boyfriend.

The little cheerleader in her head did another dance then a hip thrust in excitement.

Well, Abby was pretty darn excited about it all.

"What are you thinking about?" Tyler asked as he nipped her ear then licked her neck, rocking his erection against her ass.

"You."

"Oh, really?" he growled as he snaked his arm around her waist to palm her breast.

She panted as he took her mouth, rolling her nipple between his nimble fingers. She moaned into his mouth and wiggled her hips, aching for him.

"Hold on," he gasped. "I need to get a condom."

She gulped and bit her lip. "Only if you want one."

He froze. "What are you saying?"

"We're both clean, and I want you bare

within me."

"But what if we make a baby?"

"Then we do," she said, scared to death she was going too fast.

They weren't married, and they hadn't talked about it beyond wistful conversations of a future they both wanted to have.

Tyler smiled, a real smile that brightened his whole face. "I'd like that," he whispered.

He lifted her leg and entered her from behind, his gaze never wavering from hers. He filled her so completely that she couldn't breathe, couldn't think.

He was hers.

They made love at a leisurely pace, careful of their hurts but warming just the same. When she came, her body thrummed, and he followed soon behind her. Filling her with his seed...and maybe even their future.

Scary and thrilling to think about.

"I love you," he whispered.

"I love you, Tyler."

They lay together entwined until life called and they had to get ready, eat, and head to Jackson's. The Coopers were having a family meeting to make sure everyone was okay and to celebrate the holiday as a group before they paired off. Allison and her kids were even coming because they were part of the group, even if Brayden didn't exactly see himself as the fatherly figure.

"It's about time you showed up," Jackson said as they met him at the door.

Abby stood up on her tiptoes and kissed him lightly on the cheek. "Happy Valentine's Day, Jackson."

The stern man blushed and shook his head before squeezing her hand. "Happy Valentine's Day, Abby. I'm glad my brutish brother finally came to his senses."

"I'll toast to that," Justin said from the kitchen.

Rina laughed at his side. "It was the curse, dummy. You know he would have been on his knees long before that." She blushed beet red at her comment. "I meant begging...not...other things."

Jordan laughed and gave Abby a hug.

"Glad to see you're okay, babe."

Abby squeezed hard. "Thanks for being my witch and helping out."

Matt scowled then kissed Abby's cheek. "That's *my* witch, but she's kind of hot when she's using that magic."

Jordan rolled her eyes as Brayden shuffled over to welcome her. "Can't take those two anywhere."

"Good to see you, Bray," she said as her gaze traveled to Allison and her kids in the living room. Allison waved, but her eyes were solely on Brayden.

These two have to find each other. This is getting ridiculous.

They sat and ate together, laughing at the stupidity of being Cooper brothers, and Abby leaned into Tyler's hold, knowing this was the family she'd always wanted.

She never wanted to lose this.

"Hey, I have a present for you," Tyler whispered.

She looked up at him, and her eyes widened. "Crap, I forgot yours at the house. I thought we were doing them later."

Tyler swallowed hard and looked at his brothers. "Uh, I couldn't wait."

Okay, what was going on?

"Come with me," he said as he pulled her away from the table.

She just shrugged at their looks and went with Tyler to the foyer, away from peeping eyes and ears.

"What is it, Ty?"

"Uh, here." He handed her a rectangular box wrapped in heart-filled paper, and she rolled her eyes.

Yes, those words were so romantic.

For some reason, disappointment slid through her. She knew it was too soon, but she'd thought it would be an engagement ring. But the box didn't look like one. Plus the thing rattled.

It would be okay though. They were just starting out and had plenty of time.

She unwrapped it and laughed.

"Candy hearts?"

Really? That was it? She would have thought Tyler would have had more practice by now at the whole wooing thing.

"Open them."

Okay...

She poured a couple on her hand and froze.

One said, "*Abigail Mine.*"

While the other said, "*Marry Me.*"

Tears filled her eyes, and her hands shook, almost making her drop the box.

"Abigail?" Tyler asked, his voice shaky.

She looked up at him and couldn't breathe.

That had to be the cheesiest, most amazingly romantic thing anyone had ever done.

Oh, God, how she loved this man.

"Okay, baby. You're just crying and staring at me. Was it too soon? Too cheesy? I'll fix it. You just have to tell me what to do."

He cupped her cheeks, trying to wipe the tears that kept falling.

"Yes," she whispered. "Yes, yes, yes, yes, yes."

"Yes?"

"Yes."

"Hell yeah!" he yelled and picked her up. She almost dropped her candy.

"Hey, I don't want to drop these. I want to keep them, baby."

He set her down as the rest of the Coopers and Allison and her kids filled the alcove, talking over one another with their congratulations.

"I love you so freaking much," Tyler said as he took the box and pulled out a diamond solitaire.

Oh, this man was good.

"You're my cupid, you know that?"

"And you're my Abigail. I'm so utterly happy that I found you, Abigail. Be mine."

"I'm yours, Tyler Cooper."

He crushed his mouth to hers, and she ignored the catcalls and wolf whistles around them.

This was her happy ending. And even though it hadn't been the smoothest ride, she'd never change a thing about it.

Sometimes it took an arrow, a bad guy, and a man with wings to find happiness, but she'd take it any way she could get it.

As long as she had the Coopers and Tyler, she'd make it.

After all, it had taken a cupid to find her and make her his.

The End

Next in the Holiday, Montana world is HER LUCKY LOVE, where Brayden and Allison finally get their happy ever after...with a little luck.

ABOUT THE AUTHOR

Carrie Ann Ryan is a bestselling paranormal and contemporary romance author. After spending too much time behind a lab bench, she decided to dive into the romance world and find her werewolf mate - even if it's just in her books. Happy endings are always near - even if you have to get over the challenges of falling in love first.

Carrie Ann's Redwood Pack series is a bestselling series that has made the shifter world even more real to her and has allowed the Dante's Circle and Holiday, Montana series to be born. She's also an avid reader and lover of romance and fiction novels. She loves meeting new authors and new worlds. Any recommendations you have are appreciated. Carrie Ann lives in New England with her husband and two kittens.

www.carrieannryan.com

Also from this Author

Now Available:

Redwood Pack Series:

An Alpha's Path
A Taste for a Mate
Trinity Bound
A Night Away
Enforcer's Redemption
Blurred Expectations

Dante's Circle Series:

Dust of My Wings

Holiday, Montana Series:

Charmed Spirits
Santa's Executive
Finding Abigail

Coming Soon:

Redwood Pack

Forgiveness
Shattered Emotions

Holiday, Montana Series:

Her Lucky Love
Dreams of Ivory

Dante's Circle:

Her Warriors' Three Wishes